AIN'T SEEN MUFFIN YET

LEXY BAKER COZY MYSTERY SERIES BOOK 15

LEIGHANN DOBBS

DESCRIPTION

The Brook Ridge Falls Retirement Center is still reeling over the death of one of their own when Lexy and her senior detective friends are asked to investigate another murder. Muriel Maguire insists that her grandson, Henry, has been framed for the murder of his wife, but the clues all point to Henry, and the police already have him in custody.

The suspect list is long, including members of the victim's family who have a very unusual and suspicious profession. Too bad the husband had motive and his alibi is flimsy. Is he guilty, or is he being framed?

When the investigation leads them to a mysterious

woman, the case takes a curious twist, and a contact inside the prison reveals stunning information that turns the case on its head. Plus, there is one odd clue the police have overlooked—a corn muffin.

CHAPTER 1

The Brook Ridge Falls Retirement Center buzzed with tension as Lexy Baker put the finishing touches on a triple-tiered platter loaded with pastries. The occasion was a debate being held between the two residents running for president of the small community center inside the retirement village. Lexy was catering the event, and she wanted everything to be perfect. The last president had met with an unfortunate accident that involved one of Lexy's pies, and she was a little nervous that something might happen again. Not that the last incident had been her fault, but she didn't want to get a reputation.

Lexy adjusted a sprig of mint that decorated a tier of thickly frosted mint-chocolate bars and stood back to admire her handiwork. The hall was decorated in red, white, and blue streamers. Tables with crisp white linen tablecloths lined the side of the hall where Lexy stood. On the tables sat an assortment of Lexy's pastries as well as piles of paper plates, napkins, and plasticware. At one end was a coffee urn and Styrofoam cups.

The air was spiced with the smell of sugary pastry and percolating coffee. The muted sounds of plasticware scraping paper plates and people slurping coffee could be heard as background noise.

Gray metal folding chairs were set in rows facing the front of the room, where Lexy's grandmother's dear friend Helen stood at a wooden podium. She was wearing a smart, tailored suit in dark gray and a contrasting magenta blouse. She looked great except for the fact that the podium was a little tall for her and her head only reached just above the top.

Helen was facing off against another resident, Mario Blondini, in the retirement center's version of a presidential debate. Each was giving their speech about what they brought to the table and why the residents should vote for them.

The two had been campaigning hard for the position and had put up signs all over the retirement center grounds. There had already been two debates like this. This was the last one as voting would be in three days. Lexy couldn't figure out why they put in such an effort. It seemed like a lot of work for a position that paid no money, but maybe when you were retired, having something to do—whether it paid or not—was a big deal.

"Helen does not look happy." Mona Baker, or Nans, as Lexy called her, had come to stand beside Lexy. The senior citizen was very observant. She had to be in order to run her detective agency, and Lexy noticed that while Helen did appear composed and commanding, the lines around her mouth were a little deeper, her brow a bit more furrowed.

"Why is she unhappy?" Lexy asked.

"Mario Blondini. Just listen to him. He's one-upping her on everything!"

Lexy turned her attention to the stage where Helen was speaking.

"…and as community center president, I promise to replace those old plastic folding tables with nice new laminate ones!" Helen said.

The crowd clapped.

Mario cleared his throat and yelled above the crowd. "I promise cushioned folding chairs!"

The crowd applauded more loudly.

Mario had a smug look on his face as he glanced over at Helen, whose brows furrowed even deeper.

"Just look at the way she's cheering him on. Practically mouthing what to say at him," a voice behind Lexy whispered. She turned to see Ida and Ruth, Helen and Nans's other partners in crime-solving. Ida was nibbling on the corner of a flaky almond croissant. Ruth had her hair cut in a new silvery bob. Lexy noticed she wasn't eating any of the pastries. A few weeks ago, Ruth had been on a low-carb diet, and that hadn't worked out too well. She hoped Ruth wasn't back on it—Lexy couldn't imagine not eating pastry!

"Who?" Nans asked. "Oh, you mean Endora? She does seem a bit controlling."

Lexy glanced to the corner of the room next to Mario, where Endora Saltinado stood. From what Lexy had gathered through the gossip mill, Endora was Mario's new girlfriend. She looked quite a bit younger, especially in the tight sequined dress she was wearing. She looked like she was made up for a walk on the red carpet with her white-blond hair piled high on her head and flashy earrings and necklace. Not to mention the stilettos... Lexy couldn't even wear shoes that high, and while Endora looked young for her age, she had to be at least pushing seventy.

"She still keeps in shape, I see." Ruth had followed Lexy's gaze and was looking Endora up and down.

"Mffeew… krumbbb… yoga." Ida mumbled around her mouthful of croissant as she gestured to her own trim figure.

Lexy was used to Ida talking with food in her mouth and easily translated the garbled sentence to "we keep in shape with yoga." It was true. The four senior citizens were quite trim and spritely for their age, and that was largely due to their frequent yoga classes. While most seniors took care of their hearts for longevity reasons, Lexy suspected they did it so they could maneuver around crime scenes better. Their hobby was investigating murders, much to the dismay of Lexy's husband, police detective Jack Perillo.

"She used to be in their acrobatics show. That's how she knows Mario," Ruth said.

Lexy turned to Ruth. "Acrobatics show?"

"Mario and his family were big in the Circo Acrobata—you know, that act that travels around. It's like Cirque du Soleil with trapeze and other acrobatics, but on stage."

Naturally, Lexy was familiar with Cirque du Soleil. She squinted at the front of the room, trying to picture Mario in tights then quickly looked away, trying to replace the unpleasant image. Mario was no looker. He had bushy white hair and matching bushy eyebrows that were now frowning at Helen. He was slightly hunched over and had a bit of a paunch. His gnarled, weathered hands clutched the podium as Helen listed off the improvements she intended to make if she were elected.

"...and we'll have a coffee social the first Saturday of every month complete with pastries from the Cup and Cake." Helen nodded toward Lexy, and several people turned and clapped. Lexy's bakery, the Cup and Cake, was a popular destination among the Brook Ridge Falls retirement crowd, and she'd offered to provide the pastries at a deep discount for the Saturday socials.

"I'm going to have sandwiches *and* pastries at mine!" Mario yelled then glanced back at Endora, who nodded her approval.

"Helen is getting really mad now. Look how red her cheeks are," Nans said.

"Yeah, that Mario is very abrasive with his tactics." Ida sidled over to a tray of cream cheese brownies and selected one.

"I think he's kind of cute," Ruth said in a small voice.

Lexy, Ida, and Nans turned to stare at her. She shrugged. "What? I mean, at least he has his hair. Besides, he just lost his granddaughter, so he is likely pouring his emotions into this campaign. I'm sure he's not normally so loud and abrasive. Everyone deals with grief differently, you know."

"I suppose…" They turned their attention back to the front just as the two candidates were ending things. They managed to shake hands and thank each other. The crowd leapt up from their chairs and ran for the pastries and coffee. Helen made her way through the crowd toward them, shaking hands and smiling at folks on the way.

"Did you see that? Mario kept one-upping me!" Helen scowled across the crowd at Mario, who was talking to folks, a fake smile on his face and Endora at his side.

"He plays dirty," Nans said.

"Shameful!" Ida added.

"I still think you're the favorite," Lexy assured Helen.

"Don't worry." Ruth patted Helen's arm. "It's all going to work out just fine."

"Yeah, and look on the bright side. At least this meeting didn't end in murder." Ida glanced around at the crowd, her expression darkening when it fell on Mario. Mario glanced over at them, the smile fading from his face, menace glinting in his eyes. "Well, at least not yet."

CHAPTER 2

*L*exy and the ladies helped themselves to some pastries and stood around the coffee urn. As Ruth, Ida, Helen, and Nans chatted about the debate, Lexy was already forming her plan of attack for cleaning the place up. From her experience, the seniors loved to linger and none of them wanted to waste a pastry. She'd brought plastic containers so she could divvy up the leftovers and people could have containers to bring them home in rather than just wrap them in a napkin and shove them in their purses like Ida was so fond of doing.

A woman shuffled up to Helen. She was about five feet tall, hair in a gray bun, blue-rimmed glasses, and a sadness hovering about her. She had a Styrofoam cup of coffee in her hand.

"I saw what that Mario Blondini did to you. It was shameful," she whispered, glancing over her shoulder to make sure Mario wasn't there. "I wouldn't trust him as far as I could throw him."

This caught Lexy's attention. It sounded like the woman had prior dealings with Mario. It also caught Nans's attention. Nans leaned closer to the old lady. "Why do you say that, Muriel?"

Muriel's face crumpled, and she looked near tears. "He's the one who falsely accused my grandson Henry of murder!"

Nans leaned even closer. "Murder?"

Lexy glanced at Nans. She hadn't heard of any murder.

Muriel nodded. "I knew Henry never should have gotten involved with that girl. She was bad news from the start. They're circus folk, for crying out loud! I told him it would come to no good."

"What happened, exactly?" Ida asked.

Muriel sniffed. "They met at the Fourth of July picnic two years ago, and Henry was smitten. He never dated much, and I suppose her attentions went to his head. They married after six months!"

"And things went bad?" Ruth asked.

Muriel thought about that. "Not really. I think they were happy for a while."

"So why did he kill her?" Ida asked.

Muriel threw her hands up in the air. "That's the thing. He didn't. Sure, the police had some trumped-up evidence, and Mario pushed for it, playing the grieving grandfather all while that tartlet was hanging on his arm. It was a setup. My Henry would never murder anyone."

"But the police must have had solid evidence against him." Lexy felt like she should defend the police seeing as Jack was a detective. She was sure he would never arrest someone for murder without plenty of evidence.

"They did, but they got it wrong." Muriel took off her glasses and wiped them on a napkin then looked at Nans with tears clinging to her lashes, her eyes hopeful. "Anyway, I heard that you ladies are very good at solving murders, and I was hoping you'd look into this one."

Nans, Ruth, Ida, and Helen exchanged a look. Lexy held her breath. The four ladies had their own consulting business called the Ladies Detective Agency and had solved plenty of murders in the past. They were sought after by people who thought the police weren't solving the murders of their loved ones fast enough. They were quite good at it, too. Even Jack had asked them to consult on a few cases. Lexy was itching to look into another case, but they'd never investigated one where the police had already charged the killer. Jack might not be happy about them questioning the arrest.

"I suppose it wouldn't hurt to take a look." Nans glanced at the others, who all nodded enthusiastically.

Muriel perched her glasses back on her nose, her demeanor having brightened. "Great. Let's go back to my apartment and away from prying ears. I have some documentation from the case there that I want to show you."

Muriel's apartment was in building C of the retirement center, where Nans, Ruth, Ida, and Helen all lived. Lexy followed along, figuring the crowd could plow through more pastries in her absence and there would be less of them to clean up.

Muriel had her place decorated in 1970s senior citizen. Old maple furniture. A shag rug. Doilies. It smelled a bit like day-old cabbage. Ida wrinkled her nose but was polite enough not to say anything as they sat around the mahogany dining room table.

"Would you like coffee?"

Everyone nodded.

"Do you have any pastries to go with it?" Ida asked. The others turned to her with incredulous looks on their faces at her rudeness. Lexy wasn't surprised —Ida liked her snacks.

"I have some Lorna Dunes. Will that do?"

"Nicely," Ida said.

Muriel made the coffee and broke out some Lorna Dunes, which she spread out on a crystal plate.

Once they were all seated with steaming mugs on the table, napkins on their laps, and a cookie on each of their plates, Muriel opened the drawer of her doily-covered credenza and pulled out a manila folder. She placed it in the middle of the table and flipped it open.

The ladies all craned their necks to glimpse the contents. Nans put on her reading glasses and rifled through the sheets. Lexy was seated across the table from Nans, and even though the papers were upside down, she recognized the papers as police reports and crime scene photos. The name of the victim—Rosa Maguire—was printed at the top.

The ladies passed the papers around as they munched on the sugary shortbread cookies. Finally, Nans looked up at Muriel. "Why don't you tell us why you think your grandson is being framed."

Muriel shifted in her chair. "My Henry is a good boy. He's a doctor, sworn to protect life, not take it.

And that family." Muriel shook her head. "Well, you saw the way Mario has been acting with this election, Helen. The rest of the family is no better. I say one of them did her in for whatever reason and tried to frame Henry. He couldn't hurt a fly."

"Good point," Helen says. "Mario is shifty. He keeps replacing my signs with his! And I think he has been spying on me and somehow figured out what I was going to propose for improvements so he could do one better."

"Why would her own family kill her?" Ida dunked a Lorna Dune in her coffee.

"Who knows. They're unpredictable. Henry was at work that night. He came home and found her like that." Muriel pointed to the crime scene photo where a woman lay sprawled in a pool of blood on a kitchen floor. Lexy studied it more closely. A chair was over-turned, plates and muffins still on the table. There was a spray of blood on the cabinets.

"How was she killed?" Nans asked.

"With the very butter knife she'd used to serve butter for those muffins!" Muriel's eyes teared up.

"A butter knife?" Ruth asked. "How can you kill someone with one of those?"

"It's easy if you know the right spot." Nans pulled the photo closer to her to inspect it. "Judging by the blood spray, I'd say they got her right in the carotid artery. Even a dull knife can do damage if it's pressed hard enough. She probably bled out fast."

Helen pulled the photo in front of her. "Doesn't look like much of a struggle. The killer must have known exactly where to press. Maybe even surprised her from behind. That would take special knowledge of the anatomy, though." She looked up at Muriel. "Didn't you say Henry was a doctor?"

Muriel squirmed in her seat. "Yes."

Nans studied Muriel over the rim of her glasses. "So why do the police suspect Henry? If he was working, wouldn't he have an alibi? Where does he work?"

"He works in the emergency room at St. Mary's hospital. He was there that night, but there was some discrepancy in the timing of his alibi." Muriel looked down at her hands in her lap. "He's a good boy. He's even teaching the inmates chess. He's a model prisoner and gets to sit in the common area near the library for four hours a day because of his good behavior."

Lexy raised her left brow at Nans. Henry wouldn't be the first murderer that was lauded for good behavior. It sounded like his alibi was shaky at best. Was this just a grandmother being blinded by love for her grandson, or was there more to it?

Nans picked up the crime scene photo. "Do you mind if I keep this?"

Muriel brightened. "Not at all. Does that mean you'll take the case?"

Nans glanced at the other ladies, who all gave an imperceptible nod. "We'll study it further. It's going to be difficult, though, seeing as the police already have him in custody and we are only hearing the story secondhand from you."

"Thank you!" Muriel jumped up from her seat and ran around, giving everyone awkward hugs. "I knew you might want to hear the story straight from the horse's mouth, so I've arranged a visit with Henry this afternoon. I hate to be presumptuous, but I've already mentioned to the prison guards that his great-aunts might be accompanying me, so you can get in as family."

"Perfect." Nans took a sip of coffee. "Just let us know when, and we'll meet you there."

CHAPTER 3

They'd arranged to meet Muriel at the county jail at two p.m., so Lexy rushed back to the community center hall and cleaned up then raced to the bakery, where she somehow managed to bake a batch of chocolate chip cookies and frost two dozen cupcakes before handing over the reins to her assistant Cassie.

Cassie was more than happy to man the fort if it meant that Lexy could entertain her with tales of another of Nans and the ladies' investigations when she got back.

When Lexy arrived at the Brook Ridge Falls Retirement Center in her cheery yellow Volkswagen Beetle, the four ladies were waiting for her at the entrance to the building. Lexy noticed the grassy area out front had several signs with Helen's face on them encouraging people to vote for her.

Nans opened the passenger-side door and pushed up the seat, indicating for Ruth, Ida, and Helen to contort themselves into the back. If you're wondering how three senior citizens could maneuver themselves into the back of a VW bug, it was easy for the ladies. Their dedication to yoga kept them very flexible.

"We could have taken Ruth's car," Helen said as she settled herself in the middle. Ruth had a giant blue Oldsmobile, but Lexy preferred to drive the ladies since Ruth's driving could be dangerous not only for them but for anyone walking on the sidewalks that she often ran up onto while trying to turn.

"I don't mind driving, and this is better on gas," Lexy said.

"You know where the jail is?" Ida asked from the back corner once they were all settled inside.

Lexy had been there a time or two. "I do."

"What do you think, Mona?" Helen addressed Nans. "Do you think Henry really is innocent, or is Muriel just disillusioned?"

"Hard to say. If it was Jack who had investigated the murder, then I would highly doubt the wrong man was arrested, but I read the police report more thoroughly, and Henry and Rosa lived in New Ipswich, which is out of Jack's jurisdiction. He didn't investigate this one."

Lexy glanced at Nans. "You don't think the police are on the take, do you?"

"Or incompetent," Ruth added from the back. "My Nunzio used to tell me about many a cop that was a dunderhead. Of course, a lot of them could be bought off too."

Ruth had once dated a notorious mob boss, Nunzio Bartolli, so she knew all about corruption in the police department.

"I'm leaning toward it being something shady with those Blondinis. I wouldn't trust Mario as far as I could throw him. In fact, I think he was following me after we visited Muriel, and I thought I saw someone looking in my windows!" Helen said.

"Maybe Henry will be able to give us some clues. Looking at the papers I got from Muriel, I didn't see much concrete evidence pointing to him other than his being the obvious suspect," Nans said as Lexy pulled into the prison parking lot.

The county prison was a low brick building set in a large grassy area. There was an old dilapidated barn with a stone foundation to the left of the building and a shed farther back. Did they have prisoners working in there? Lexy wasn't sure of what they would be doing. The whole place was surrounded by a metal fence with barbed wire at the top. She supposed it would be difficult to escape even if you were in a farmwork duty program on the grounds.

Muriel was waiting in front of the steel-and-glass doors. Lexy found a spot close to the front, and they all piled out.

"I really appreciate this." Muriel opened the door and gestured for them to step inside. "I think you'll agree about my Henry once you get to meet him."

The lobby had plain white walls and white-and-green tiled flooring that hadn't been updated in fifty years. Their footsteps echoed on the tile as they approached the oak divider to talk to the guard that sat behind it. It looked clean, but Lexy couldn't help but detect a faint hint of desperation and hopelessness mixed in with the smell of lemon cleaner.

"You here for your visit, Muriel?" the guard, a gray-haired man whose green prison uniform fit him a bit tightly, asked. Apparently, Muriel was well-known here.

"Yes, I've brought some of Henry's great-aunts. It's all been cleared by the warden." Muriel sounded confident—apparently, she must have some pull.

A buzzer sounded, and Muriel walked over to a steel door with a small window and pulled it open like she knew the routine. The guard met them on the other side and walked them down a hallway.

Lexy expected to be led past rows of jail cells, but instead the guard turned down a corridor and they walked past a small library and a room with a long table, orange plastic chairs, two sofas, and a few reading chairs.

"That's the prison library and the common area where Henry teaches chess." Muriel gestured toward a small table that had a chessboard, its ivory and ebony pieces in play.

Beyond the common area was another steel door with a small square window in the middle. The window was thick glass with a grid of wires. The guard buzzed the door open to reveal a plain room painted light gray. The only thing inside was a long metal table with navy-blue plastic chairs around it. The chairs were arranged with one single chair on the far side, two at each end, and four along the near side.

"Well, have a seat." Muriel gingerly pulled out one of the chairs, and the rest of them followed her lead, leaving a chair empty on one side of the table for Henry.

"I don't know why they don't paint these rooms a cheerier color." Helen huffed as she adjusted her skirt. "No wonder everyone in prison is depressed."

"They could use some snacks too. I bet that would cheer people up," Ida added.

"At least coffee," Nans said.

Luckily the door opened again before the ladies could postulate any further about how they would revamp the visitation process, and a man in an orange jumpsuit was led in. He was in his early thirties, with dark-brown hair and a thin mustache and wearing wire-rim glasses. His eyes lit up when he saw Muriel but then narrowed with suspicion at the rest of them.

Muriel jumped up. "Henry! I brought your great-aunts to see you!"

With all the winking and head tilting that Muriel was doing, it was a wonder the guard didn't suspect that she was lying. Then again, Lexy didn't know if he really cared. They were just harmless old ladies, or so everyone thought. Nans always said that one of the advantages of being a senior citizen was that most people took no notice of you.

"Thanks, Gram," Henry said uncertainly as he took the lone seat on the opposite side of the table.

"You got fifteen minutes." The guard shut the door as he left.

Muriel leaned toward Henry and whispered, "These are my neighbors that do the investigations. They're going to help you."

Henry still looked a little suspicious of them. Was that because he wasn't confident that a bunch of white-haired old ladies could help, or because maybe he wasn't as innocent as Muriel thought?

"The police seem to think they have a good case." Henry took an ebony chess piece out of his pocket, his fingers running over the smooth contours as he tapped it nervously on the table.

"Why don't you tell us what happened," Nans said.

Henry took a deep breath and let it out slowly then leaned back and started talking. "I was working that night. I work in the emergency room."

"And you came right home and found her?" Nans knew this wasn't the truth but wanted to see what Henry would say.

Henry leaned forward and placed the chess piece on the table then started turning it over and over like one might turn an hourglass after the sand has run out. "No. I lost a patient. Car accident. I had to drive around a bit to clear my head."

"So you drove around and then came home and found Rosa dead," Ruth said.

Henry's lips pressed into a tight line. He kept flipping the chess pieces over to one side then the other. "Yep."

"And you can't prove your alibi because no one was with you in the car," Nans said.

Henry nodded.

"That doesn't sound like much of a reason to arrest you," Helen said. "Surely the police have some solid evidence against you."

"Well, there *is* the life insurance motive, and I can't prove my whereabouts."

"Life insurance?" Nans gave Muriel a raised-brow look.

Muriel blushed. "Did I forget to mention that?"

Henry continued to work the chess piece. "Rosa had a big policy because she still performed in the Circo Acrobata from time to time. She was a trapeze artist, and as you can imagine, it's a bit dangerous. She wanted to make sure I was taken care of."

"How much?" Nans asked.

"One million."

Ruth whistled. "That's a lot of motive…"

Henry stopped working the chess piece and looked at Ruth with hard eyes. "I did. Not. Kill her."

Ruth held her hands up. "Woah, now. We're here to help. Do you know anyone who might have wanted to kill her?"

Henry studied the chess piece. "Everyone loved

Rosa, but recently she had something on her mind. Something to do with her family."

Muriel huffed. "No surprise there. You ask me, *they* are behind this."

"Why would her family want to kill her?" Helen asked.

"I have no idea. She always said she loved them, even those who weren't really related. You see, Rosa and the Blondinis considered everyone in the Circo Acrobata their family."

"You've seen how Mario acts even with something like the election for community center president," Muriel said. "He's got no conscience. And don't even get me started on that new girlfriend of his."

Henry made a face. "I'm not sure about her, either. But she's part of the family because she was in the Circo."

"What did Mario do in this circus?" Lexy asked.

Henry started turning the chess piece over again. "Trapeze. He was still working until a few years ago. All that working with his hands made him strong but also gave him arthritis, and he had to quit. I think he's still a bit angry about that."

Angry, or jealous? Lexy wondered. *Could he be jealous of his family still able to work? Would he kill his own granddaughter over that?* It didn't seem possible, so she dismissed that idea as soon as it came to her.

"What about Endora? What did she do?" Ruth asked.

"Mostly acrobatics. Some high wire. They do everything from knife throwing to plate spinning to magic acts. Endora sort of filled in where she was needed." Henry sighed. "Anyway, I don't see how any of this will help me."

"If we can figure out the means, motive, or opportunity, then that might help us narrow suspects down." Nans snapped open her large patent leather purse and took out a piece of paper. "Unfortunately so far, you have all three."

She put the paper on the table and slid it to Henry. It was the photo of the crime scene. He looked down and grimaced, clearly affected by the sight of his wife's body. Was he saddened about it, or did he feel guilty because he'd caused it?

"Now, I know this might be hard to look at, but I want you to tell me if you see anything out of place here," Nans said.

Henry fiddled with the chess piece nervously as he studied the picture. "Well, there's Rosa laying there like that. She must have known her killer because the table is set, and... I guess the killer brought muffins."

"Really?" Ida craned her neck to look at the photo. "How do you know the killer brought them?"

"We never have stuff like that in the house, and there weren't any muffins when I left. Near as I can figure, someone came to visit and brought them." Henry pointed to the table in the photo. "You can see Rosa had it all set up nice for a visit and instead..."

Something about the photo made Lexy take a closer look. It wasn't the melted butter or the butter knife lying in the blood or even the overturned chair. It was the golden-yellow muffins. They were corn muffins, and there was something unusual about them.

"These muffins are kind of strange." Lexy pointed to the tops of the muffins in the picture, where large sugar crystals glistened. "These have sugar crystals on top."

"I love when muffins have those." Ida closed her eyes and smacked her lips together. "I can practically taste the sugary crunch now."

"Yeah, but have you ever seen them on *corn* muffins?" Lexy asked.

Ida's eyes flew open. "Now that you mention it, I haven't."

Nans snapped her fingers. "That's right! It's very unusual. I bet not too many bakeries do that."

"I don't know of any that do," Lexy added.

"So?" Henry asked.

"This could help us find the killer." Nans put the paper back in her purse. "If we can find the bakery that makes these, maybe they will remember who bought them."

The door flew open, and the guard poked his head in. "Time's up!"

Henry sighed and stood. "Sounds kind of flimsy to me."

Nans gave him a look. "You have any better ideas?"

"No." Henry let the guard lead him away, and they all filed out of the room. Lexy wasn't sure if they were supposed to wait for the guard to show them out or leave on their own. Nans must have been too excited to wait, as she plowed forward clutching her purse.

"See, I told you he was innocent," Muriel said.

"It certainly gives us something to look into." Nans turned the corner leading to the library.

"Do you really think someone at the bakery will remember who they sold muffins to weeks ago?" Ruth asked.

Nans shrugged. "No idea. We might get lucky. It's a lead, and we always follow all leads."

Just then, an inmate wearing an orange jumpsuit like Henry's crossed their path on the way to the library. He was pushing a metal tray of library books. He turned to look at them, then his face broke into a snaggle-toothed smile.

"Ruth? Is that you?"

Ruth squinted at the man then grinned. "Vinny! What are you doing here?"

Vinny's smile faded. "Got pinched on a heist. I think someone ratted me out."

"Oh, that's too bad." Ruth turned to the others. "Everyone, this is Nunzio's cousin, Vinny."

Ruth introduced them all. Muriel seemed a bit reluctant to shake Vinny's hand, but who could blame her, considering he was one of the inmates.

Vinny seemed pleasant enough, even though he was apparently some sort of robber. He explained more, as if he were proud of the heist he'd been incarcerated for. "You might have heard of the Broadmoore Heist? Yeah, that was me. Well, me and some others."

"Wasn't that the mansion that got broken into about six months ago?" Ruth asked.

Vinny nodded then leaned closer to her and

lowered his voice. "They still haven't figured out how we did it."

"So do you have the loot hidden somewhere?" Ida asked. "I heard they never found it."

Vinny's face darkened. "That's the thing. We were letting it cool off before we could fence it, and then someone ratted me out. I don't think I'm going to get my share."

Helen's brow shot up. "Is that why they told on you, so they could keep it for themselves?"

Vinny pressed his lips together and stroked his chin as if newly considering this. "Could be."

"What's with the cart?" Ida asked.

Vinny puffed up with pride. "I run the library. I get perks because of good behavior, so I get to take the books back and forth to the other inmates. You'd be surprised how many of us like to read."

"I'm sure we would." Nans started back down the hall. "Well, nice to meet you, Vinny. We gotta run."

"Jeez, Ruth, you do have an interesting network of acquaintances," Helen said. "I don't want to consort with too many felons though. Might harm my chances of winning the election."

Ruth gave Helen a hard look. "What's that supposed to mean?"

"Now ladies, no fighting," Nans said as they

approached the door that led to the lobby. "Having someone on the inside might prove useful."

The door buzzed, and Nans opened it and stepped into the lobby, stopping short just a few steps in and causing everyone else to skid to a stop.

Lexy's heart tumbled when a familiar voice said, "Please tell me I'm not seeing who I think I am seeing."

Jack! Darn it! Sometimes he wasn't too keen on Lexy joining Nans's unconventional investigations, and Lexy was sure he wouldn't be too happy to find her at the prison. She peeked out from behind Nans, a sheepish look on her face. "Hi, sweetie."

Jack pursed his lips. "What are you doing here?"

Helen cleared her throat. "I brought them here to help me with my campaign."

Jack looked doubtful. "At the prison? I thought you were running for president of the senior center."

"I am. But the more votes, the better. Some of the people in here have relatives who might vote for me." Helen gestured toward Muriel to prove her point.

Jack crossed his arms over his chest. "You expect me to believe that?"

Nans glanced at the vintage Seiko on her wrist. "Oh, look at the time. We have to run! So great to see you, Jack!" She rushed past Jack with the others following.

As Lexy hurried behind them, Jack caught her by the elbow. "I'll talk to you later at home."

His face was stern, but his velvety brown eyes were soft. He might be a little mad, but Lexy was sure he'd get over it, hopefully before dinner.

"Great! I'll be looking forward to that. Love you!" Lexy rose up on her toes and gave him a peck on the cheek before escaping out the door as fast as she could.

CHAPTER 4

Nans and the rest of the ladies could barely wait for Lexy to pull to a stop in the parking lot of the Brook Ridge Falls Retirement Center before they were pushing open the doors and jumping out. They were eager to get up to Nans's apartment and go over the clues.

"Uh oh." Ruth pointed toward the lawn in front of the building. "Do you see what I see?"

All of the campaign signs that Helen had put up on the lawn in front of the building had been replaced with Mario's signs.

"I *told* you he was replacing my signs!" Helen stormed over and started pulling the signs out.

"Helen! I'm so glad I caught you!" Norm Rosen

hurried up the sidewalk and Helen straightened, plastering a smile on her face.

"Hello, Norm. So lovely to see you."

"Yes, yes indeed. I just wanted to tell you that your idea for expanding the library at the community center is a grand one. You have my vote."

"Why, thank you very much, Norm." Helen beamed at him, placing herself strategically in front of Mario's signs so as to block them.

"Well, have a nice day!" Norm trotted off.

Helen went back to pulling out the signs. "See that? The people want to vote for *me*. They can tell that Mario is a shady liar!"

"Hey! What are you doing? Leave those signs alone!" Mario rushed up and grabbed the sign out of Helen's hands. "What do you think you are doing, pulling out my signs?"

"*Your* signs? Mine were here first and *you* pulled them out!" Helen said.

Endora, who had slithered up beside Mario, butted in, "You hogged the whole lawn! You put all your signs here and there was no room for others. It's only fair that you guys share the space."

"Yeah, fair's fair." A slim man in his mid-thirties with dark, greasy hair and a scraggly beard stood beside Endora. "You better watch who you mess with."

Mario ripped the sign out of Helen's hands, almost smacking Endora in the face. Luckily, Endora had quick reflexes and she turned her face, narrowly avoiding the edge of the sign. Good thing, too, as a slice from the side of that thick poster paper would have made for a nasty paper cut. But judging by the scars Lexy could now see on Endora's chin and cheek, it appeared as if Endora was used to avoiding things hitting her in the face. Perhaps that was from being part of the acts in the Circo Acrobato.

"Fine, then. I'll take this side of the lawn." Helen pointed to the left of the front door. "And you take the other. Won't make any difference, anyway. The residents all seem to favor voting for me."

"Ha!" Mario stalked over to the left of the door and planted the sign in the ground. "They won't want to vote for you after they see the types of people you consort with."

"What are you talking about?" Helen frowned at Nans, Lexy, Ruth, and Ida. "My friends here are the most upstanding citizens. Well, maybe except for Ruth…"

"Not them. That Maguire woman. Her grandson murdered my granddaughter." Mario's dark eyes glistened with hatred. "Yeah, don't think I didn't see you conspiring with her. I know you ladies are up to no good, and don't think you'll get away with it. That boy is a killer, and don't you think that you're going to use some of your influence with the police to get him out of it." Mario shoved the sign into the ground with great effort then rubbed his hands.

"We'll see about that! Besides, we don't use our influence, we prove cases on clues and facts." Helen turned to Lexy and the others. "Come on, ladies. We have work to do!"

She stomped off toward the door with the others following. Ida paused to throw a dirty look in Mario's direction.

"Can you believe the nerve of him?" Helen said as they traversed the hallway to Nans's apartment.

"He does seem to think that Henry is guilty," Nans said.

"Is that what you think?" Ida asked.

"Not sure yet. We have to explore all angles." Nans rummaged in her purse for the key. It took a while because the oversized purse was full of items. She pulled out a flashlight, Kleenex, a small can of peas, and several rain bonnets, handing them all to Ruth as she fished inside for the key. Finally, she pulled it out and unlocked the door.

Nans's apartment was a spacious two-bedroom overlooking the woods. The living room, with its microsuede sectional, was to the right of the door. The dining room, with the large mahogany table where the ladies usually sat to discuss their investigations, was to the right. The dining room was open to the kitchen beyond, and Lexy could see the white cabinets and cheery red nicknacks on the dark granite counters.

"I'll get the whiteboard. We're gonna need it for this one." Nans headed toward the spare bedroom, where she kept the six-foot-tall rolling whiteboard.

"I'll put on coffee." Helen headed toward the kitchen, where Ida was already picking through the fridge.

"I wish we'd brought some snacks." Ida looked over her shoulder pointedly at Lexy. Normally, Lexy would bring a batch of pastries from her bakery, but this time, she hadn't had a chance to stop there.

"There are some Oreos in the cabinet," Nans said as she pulled the board into the dining room.

Lexy and Ruth set the table with Nans's delicate flowered dessert plates, a crystal creamer, sugar, and cloth napkins with pink embroidered edges.

Soon, the enticing smell of percolating coffee permeated the room, and they were seated around the table with steaming mugs full of the dark brew. All except for Ida—she had a glass of milk.

Nans put her mug on the table and stood at the whiteboard. "This case is a little different than our usual. I don't think we've ever had a case where the suspect is incarcerated and the police are no longer investigating."

Ida grabbed an Oreo from the serving platter in the middle of the table and dipped it in her milk. "I don't believe we have, but we're at a disadvantage because all the clues have been found and all the suspects have been interrogated. The case isn't fresh like it usually is when we come on board, and we don't know what the police know."

"I can ask Jack," Lexy offered. While Jack didn't like them investigating his cases, she had a few ways of getting information out of him without it being obvious.

"He wasn't the investigating detective, but maybe he'll know something." Nans turned to the white-board. "All we know is that Henry claims he came home and found Rosa dead. His alibi can't be verified."

"The killer had some sort of skill that enabled them to kill her with the butter knife." Ruth reached for an Oreo. Apparently her low-carb restriction really was over. Though Lexy wondered if she'd ever stuck to it, seeing as they'd discovered her hiding pie crust in her purse. At least now she was eating carbs out in the open.

"And most likely knew Rosa since they brought the muffins and she had the table set for a friendly social visit," Ida added.

"It's too bad we don't really have any suspects other than 'someone who knew her.' That's too broad." Ruth pulled the Oreo apart and licked the creamy middle. "I could pump Vinny for information. You know how those inmates talk to each other. Maybe Henry said something."

Nans considered that. "Maybe, but I don't think we can just waltz into the prison and talk to inmates. We'll save that for a last resort."

"Muriel mentioned that the Blondinis could be behind it, and I wouldn't put it past them. Did you see how mean Mario looked when he mentioned it? Sure, he pretended to be upset, but I think he was putting on an act. I'm not saying he killed his own granddaughter, but maybe it was someone in the family and he's protecting them," Helen said. "Henry did mention that Rosa had a concern about her family."

"What about that creepy guy that was with them

today? I bet he's the killer." Ida crunched into an Oreo. "Who was that guy anyway?"

"One of their cousins, I believe," Nans said. "He's in the Circo act. But we can't just go making assumptions about people because of the way they look. What motive would he have?"

"When Henry said Rosa was worried about something to do with her family, he might not have been referring to her actual blood relatives. Remember how the Blondinis consider anyone in the Circo Acrobata as family?" Ruth narrowed her gaze at Helen. "And let's not go accusing Mario just because you are in competition with him for the president slot. He has kind eyes."

"Kind eyes?" Helen looked incredulous. "They look like the black soulless eyes of a snake to me!"

"It could still be Henry." Ida picked another Oreo off the plate and dunked. "He's a doctor and would know just where to shove the knife in to hit that artery just right. The killer would have to know that because otherwise they'd risk her getting away in the struggle. I mean, with something like a butter knife, you have to be quick and accurate."

"He did stand to gain money with the life insurance," Helen pointed out.

"Good point," Ruth said. "And he has that flimsy

alibi. Plus, he seems kind of sketchy to me. He was nervous when we questioned him too. Did you see the way he was playing with that pawn?"

"You mean the chess piece?" Ida asked. "That was a knight."

"No, the knight is the horse," Helen said. "The piece he had was the bishop. That's the one that goes diagonal."

"No, that's the queen," Ida said.

"No." Helen shook her head. "The queen goes diagonal and up and down, but only one square at a time."

Ruth waved her hand. "Whatever. My point is that he was fiddling with it like he was nervous."

Nans tapped her marker on the whiteboard. "Ladies! We have work to do!"

Everyone turned their attention to Nans, and she uncapped the marker. The noxious smell of white-board marker drifted over as she started to write on the board.

"Now we need a way to verify the alibi. Maybe Lexy can find out more about that from Jack." Nans lifted a brow at Lexy, and Lexy nodded. She'd do her best. Nans turned back to the board. "We don't really have anything that points to one suspect, so we need to find out who brought those muffins."

"How will we do that?" Ruth asked.

"I can only think of one way. Those muffins are rare, so we need to visit the bakeries near Henry and Rosa's place. If we find one that has those muffins, we might get lucky and they might remember who buys them." Nans turned to Ruth. "Henry and Rosa lived in New Ipswich. Can you see if there are any bakeries in town?"

Ruth whipped an iPad out of her purse, perched a pair of magenta-framed glasses on her nose, and started typing. "There's the Confection Connection over on Elm Street."

Nans wrote the bakery name and street on the board.

"And Doughy Delights over on Spring Street..." Ruth scrolled down the screen. "And Sugar Daddies on the edge of town on Granville." She looked up at Nans over the rims of her glasses. "That's it for New Ipswich, but there are others in the next town."

Nans finished writing the names on the whiteboard then turned to them. "We'll start with these and then branch out."

Ida shot out of her chair and grabbed her purse. "Great, I could use a cupcake. Let's go."

Ruth waved her back into her seat. "Wait a minute. Do you really think that someone is going to remember exactly who they sold corn muffins to? And what if they sold to more than one person? Do bakery owners know the names of every single person that buys muffins?" Ruth glanced at Lexy.

"Well, no, but we do have our regulars. I know many of my customers as well as their favorite pastries," Lexy said.

"That's right," Nans said. "We might get lucky because corn muffins with sugar crystals on top are very unusual. Seems like something someone would come back for over and over again. We don't have many other leads right now, so we might as well follow this one."

"Good thinking." Ida shot up from her chair again.

"Not so fast." Nans gestured for Ida to sit, and she did so, a look of extreme annoyance on her face. "It's almost five o'clock, and the bakeries might be closed. Besides, we have the potluck dinner tonight, and Helen wants to be there to get more votes. I say we meet here at ten a.m. tomorrow and start to case these bakeries then. That will give Lexy time to glean information from Jack. If she learns anything new, it might change our course of action."

*L*exy arrived at home that night with a box of leftover pastries she'd salvaged when she'd swung by the Cup and Cake to help Cassie close up. It was Jack's turn to cook, and she found him out back preparing the grill for the steaks. Just the though of those slabs of N.Y. sirloin sizzling on the flame made her stomach growl.

Sprinkles, her white Shih Tzu mix, tore herself away from staring intently at the grill to bound around Lexy's ankles until Lexy picked her up. She petted the dog's silky fur and accepted wet kisses on her cheek.

"How was your day?" Jack kissed her other cheek. Since he was over six feet, he towered over

Lexy and had to lean over to do it. "I mean, other than your little visit to the jail."

A blush crept into Lexy's cheeks, and she focused on putting Sprinkles onto the ground gently. "Oh that. Yeah… well, you know how Nans gets when she gets a bee in her bonnet."

Jack put the marinated steaks on and flames lept up. "So, what is she into this time?"

Lexy set the glass-top patio table as she told Jack about Muriel Maguire's request that instigated the visit to Henry. By the time she was done, they were both seated at the table and their plates full of steak, baked potato, and salad. Glasses of wine sat on the table in front of them. "I think Nans might be on to something though. There was a clue at the crime scene that might shed some light, and I doubt the police followed up on it."

Jack looked up from buttering his corn. "What makes you think the police didn't follow up? I assume the murder happened out of my jurisdiction since the case isn't familiar."

"It happened in New Ipswich." Lexy stabbed a tomato wedge with her fork and looked at Jack from under her lashes. "I'm sure *you* would have caught this, but it's something a lot of police might not have. The killer brought muffins."

Jack's lips quirked in amusement. "Muffins? That should narrow down the suspect pool considerably. And why couldn't Henry have brought those himself?"

"Well, he could have, I suppose, except he works late at the hospital, and the bakeries would be closed by the time he got out."

"Even so, how are muffins going to help you prove anything?"

"They were unusual muffins. Corn muffins with sugar crystals on top. Hardly anyone does that. I should know." Lexy cut off a small piece of steak and savored the tangy morsel as Jack considered what she was telling him.

Sprinkles, who had been sitting at her feet and staring at every forkful, must have decided Lexy wasn't going to drop anything, so she took up position at Jack's feet. He bent down to scratch her behind the ears. "So you're thinking that you can find out who sells these rare muffins and then figure out who bought them? Sounds like a long shot. No wonder the police didn't follow up on that."

Lexy was a little insulted at Jack's dismissal. It made her more determined to prove the muffins were a viable clue and to solve the case. Nans was very good at solving cases, and she'd find the real killer.

Unless it really was Henry. Lexy still hadn't ruled that out. "There's something else too."

"What?" Jack's eyes were wary as he studied her over the rim of his wine glass. They'd been together for a while now, and apparently, he knew when she was going to ask for a favor.

"Henry says he has an alibi, but the police arrested him anyway. He's an emergency room doctor and was at work that night. He lost a patient and then drove around a bit to decompress, but the timing is so tight. Anyway, it seems like whoever investigated just wanted to close the case fast." Lexy gave Jack her most flirtatious look. "Maybe you could look into the case and see if you notice anything that seems odd?"

Jack took a sip of wine then smiled. "Okay, I can take a look, but I think you and Nans might be in for a disappointment. I'm sure the police had good reason to arrest Henry."

"Nans won't stop investigating until she sees that for herself." Lexy speared a piece of lettuce and shoved it in her mouth.

"That's why I'm going to look into it. The sooner Nans and the ladies are convinced the right killer is in jail, the sooner they will drop this. There's one condition, though."

Darn it! Lexy hated conditions, but they needed

Jack's help if they wanted insight into the police investigation. "What?"

"No more going to the jail to visit with inmates."

Lexy considered the condition. They'd already talked to Henry, so they probably wouldn't need another trip to the jail, and even if they did maybe she could stay in the car so as to not break her promise. Finding out the insider information from the police was critical, so she didn't have much choice. She smiled and reached her hand across the table to shake on it. "Deal."

CHAPTER 6

*L*exy got to the bakery bright and early the next morning. She had to meet Nans at ten and wanted enough time to get the morning baking done and everything set up before leaving Cassie alone for the morning. It would be easier for Cassie if she could focus on waiting on customers and not have to run back into the kitchen to check on things in the oven.

Lexy was bent over the oven, taking out a batch of whoopie pie cakes when Cassie came in through the back door. She picked a pink gingham vintage apron off the pegs where several were hanging by the back door. Lexy smiled at the contrast of Cassie's nose ring, multi-studded earlobes, and aqua-tipped spiked hair against the old-fashioned gingham apron.

"I've been dying to find out about this case you guys are on," Cassie said as she pulled ingredients for blueberry muffins—milk, blueberries, butter—out of the fridge. At the Cup and Cake, they typically baked fresh pastries at various times during the day when the cafe was slow, but in the mornings, they always made fresh muffins for the morning crowd.

"This one's a little different because the police think they already have the killer in custody." Lexy told her about the case, including their visit to jail and the current theory about the corn muffins, while she mixed up cream, vanilla, and sugar for the whipped filling for the middle of the whoopie pies.

"The victim was in the Circo Acrobata? Have you seen the show?" Cassie asked.

"No." Lexy tested the cakes to see if they'd cooled enough then flipped them upside down and started spreading the filling. "Is it like a circus? Muriel Maguire mentioned something about trapezes and stuff."

"Sort of. They have high-wire acts, trapezes, and lots of dance and acrobatics. Good music. It's kind of classy, like that Cirque du Soleil show in Vegas."

"Really? It's hard to picture Mario Blondini doing anything classy. Helen was so mad at him yesterday I thought she was going to spit."

Cassie grinned. "Is the presidential race getting heated?"

"Yeah. You'd think they were running for president of the country, not just the community center."

Cassie carefully poured the batter into Teflon muffin cups. "Well, I hope she wins. I wouldn't want Blondini in there. In fact, I thought it was odd he was running. Guess he's bored since he retired from the show. But part of me wonders if he's up to something. I've heard rumors."

Lexy was all ears. "What kinds of rumors?"

"Oh, just that maybe they were involved in some shady stuff. Like that big heist that happened a few months ago."

"Really? Ruth ran into an old friend of Nunzio's when we visited the prison, and he mentioned something about a heist." Maybe Ruth's idea about talking to Vinny wasn't so far-fetched. Too bad Lexy had promised Jack she wouldn't go to the jail.

"Well, it's just rumor. Probably nothing to it." Cassie put the blueberry muffins in the oven and started on a batch of chocolate chocolate chip.

Lexy thought about that as she finished up the whoopie pies. Could the heist be related to Rosie's murder? And if so, did it have something to do with the Blondinis? Henry had said that Rosa was worried about something to do with family. But if Rosa was in on the heist, wouldn't Henry have known? Maybe she was trying to keep it from him and he found out. Would that make him mad enough to kill her?

Lexy put the whoopie pies on a paper-doily-lined tray then untied her apron—vintage cherries—and slipped it over her head. Smoothing her navy-blue t-shirt over her faded jeans, she glanced at the clock.

"I'm supposed to meet Nans and the ladies at ten. We're going to scope out some of the bakeries local to the scene of the crime to see if any of them sell corn muffins with sugar crystals." Lexy was excited about scoping out the other bakeries. She always liked to compare other bakeries to her own. Sometimes it gave her good ideas for new pastries or how to arrange them, and others, it just made her feel proud that her bakery was the nicest one in the area.

"Sounds like fun. Today should be an easy day since it's mid-week. I'll man the fort."

Lexy picked up the tray of whoopie pies and headed toward the front part of the bakery where the pastry cases and cafe tables were. "I was hoping you'd say that. I'll just put these in the case and open the shop on my way out."

～

Lexy arrived at Nans's twenty minutes later carrying a white bakery box filled with pastries she'd taken from her bakery. She knew they were going to be visiting plenty of bakeries that day, but Ida would have a conniption if Lexy showed up empty-handed.

Ida answered the door and promptly relieved Lexy of the box, slipping the lid open and peeking in on the way to the dining room table, where everyone was sipping coffees.

"Hi, dear." Nans gestured toward an empty chair. "Have a seat. Ruth was just mapping out our route to the Confection Connection."

Lexy sat while Ida piled the pastries on a platter. Ida took an almond croissant for herself and then passed the tray around.

"So, did you find out anything interesting from Jack?" Nans asked.

"He wasn't familiar with the case but said he'd look into it," Lexy said. "I did find out something interesting from Cassie, though."

Nans paused the bran muffin she'd chosen halfway to her mouth. "Oh? Do tell."

Lexy picked a snickerdoodle from the pastry tray and broke off a small piece. "She said she heard some rumor that the circus the Blondinis belonged to was involved in some heist."

Ruth perked up. "The heist that sent Vinny to the can?"

Nans looked at Ruth. "The can? What kind of talk is that? I think you hung around with Nunzio too much."

Ruth pulled out her iPad. "I told you we should go back and talk to Vinny. He could be a wealth of information. Let's see what I can find out about this heist."

"In light of this new news, maybe we should add a visit to Vinny to our list," Nans said.

Lexy broke off a bigger piece of cookie. "Jack made me promise I wouldn't go back to the prison. It was a condition of him looking into the case." She shoved the piece of cookie into her mouth.

Nans made a face. "Oh. Well, we wouldn't want you to go back on a promise. Maybe we'll go without you if we deem it necessary."

"There's only one heist I can find mentioned here," Ruth said as she tapped on the surface of the iPad. "The Broadmoore Heist. You know, that big mansion on the hill with the great mountain view."

"I heard about that," Helen said. "Someone stole a bunch of antiques, and the police have no leads."

"No leads?" Ida looked interested. "Maybe we should expand our repertoire and solve that case too." The ladies normally only solved murder cases, but

Lexy could see by the way they were considering it they wouldn't mind branching out into burglaries.

"Let's just focus on the one we have for now," Nans said. "But maybe after we solve Rosa's murder, if nothing else of interest comes up, we can solve that case too."

"The two might be related if the Blondinis did have something to do with the heist," Lexy said. "What did they steal?"

"Just some vases and paintings. Old ones worth a lot," Ruth said. "Doesn't seem very smart to me. It's hard to sell that stuff because it's too recognizable. At least that's what Nunzio told me."

"Even more reason it could be the Blondinis," Helen said. "They aren't that smart."

"Good point." Nans started clearing the table. "We'll keep that under consideration. For now, though, I say we get over to the Confection Connection. The sooner we find the place that sells those muffins, the sooner we can cross that clue off our list."

CHAPTER 7

The Confection Connection was a small bakery with a pink-and-white awning. The awning was cute, but Lexy noticed right away that they had no cafe tables and no coffee station. Hardly competition for her place.

Ida and Lexy stood at the bakery case, inspecting the pastries.

"The frosting is kind of skimpy on those cupcakes." Ida pointed to a row of cupcakes that, in Lexy's opinion, were barely frosted. She always tried to put at least an inch of frosting on hers, and these barely had a quarter of that.

"I agree," Lexy whispered. "And look at how small the brownies are."

Lexy always cut giant four-by-four-inch brownies

at the Cup and Cake, and the ones in this case were more like bite-size pieces.

"They're tiny!" Ida hissed as she sidled over toward the counter. "I better order a sampling of some of these for taste-testing purposes."

While Ida ordered, Lexy joined Nans at the muffin case. They had corn muffins but none with sugar crystals.

"Excuse me," Nans called to the clerk who was ringing up Ida. "Do you have corn muffins with sugar crystals on top?"

The clerk made a face. "Sugar crystals? No. That's gross."

"Not necessarily," Nans said. "I love the little crunch those crystals make. Of course, one has to be careful not to break a tooth. Has anyone ever ordered some with those on them?"

The clerk shook her head. "No. I would remember that. Not sure I would even do it. They have to be put on when the muffins are hot in order to stick. Are you ladies going to buy something?"

Nans scanned the pastry case. "Umm... I'll have a lemon square and a molasses cookie."

"They're kind of small... better get two," Ida whispered.

"I think I'll stick with one. Trying to watch my weight." Nans turned to Ruth and Helen, who were over by the window. "Do you want anything, Ruth? Helen?"

"No thanks," they chorused.

By the time Nans paid for her purchase, Ida had already devoured a brownie and was halfway into a cupcake. She leaned over toward Lexy and lowered her voice. "Not nearly as good as yours."

Lexy was heartened by the compliment, but the warm feeling burst when Helen gasped and pointed at the window. "Would you look at who's out there! I bet he followed us!"

Lexy glanced out to see Mario Blondini and Endora walking away. Endora was munching on a chocolate cookie, and she glanced back with a smirk as Helen tapped loudly on the window.

Helen watched them walk away, her eyes blazing with fury. "Well, I never! He's moved my signs, he's piggybacking on my ideas, and now he's following me? The nerve!"

At Ida's insistence, they stopped off at the Cup and Cake on the way back to Nans's. She said she needed some good pastries to get rid of the taste from the Confection Connection.

Cassie was done with the morning's baking and pulled the fresh pastries from the case for them as they filled her in on their trip to the Confection Connection.

"I don't think it's anywhere near as nice as the Cup and Cake," Helen said, taking the piece of red velvet cake she'd ordered over to the coffee station and pouring a dark roast into one of the white stoneware mugs that Lexy kept for customers to use.

"The portions are too small there." Ida took a chocolate-frosted brownie from Cassie and headed toward the cafe table near the window.

"That place is no competition for you." Ruth patted Cassie's hand as she took an almond scone. "You girls have nothing to worry about."

Lexy split a blonde brownie with Cassie and then sat at the table where the ladies were getting settled with their pastries and coffees. The ladies were right —that other bakery couldn't hold a candle to the Cup and Cake, especially with its scenic view of the waterfall across the street and the planter boxes over-flowing with flowers lined up on the bridge railing. Lexy had been lucky to get this spot and even luckier to be able to put her cafe tables at the window and outside on the wide sidewalk that overlooked the falls.

Lexy picked at the blondie as she watched Nans put the lemon square and molasses cookies she'd gotten from Cassie next to the ones she'd bought at the Confection Connection.

"These are much smaller than Lexy's." Pride swelled in Lexy's chest as Nans pointed to the Confection Connection pastries, which were about half the size of hers.

"They're puny! And the cookie doesn't look as moist." Helen sank her fork through the thick layer of frosting and into the red velvet cake.

"I bet the lemon is tart." Ruth made a sour face.

"I'll take one for the team and taste-test it." Ida grabbed the lemon square, put it in her mouth, and made a big show of chewing while making sour faces. "Yep, too tart."

The bells jangled, and Jack walked in.

"Hey. I was hoping to find you all here." He gave Lexy a quick peck on the cheek before continuing on to the coffee carafes. "I'm just picking up some coffees to go for me and John."

John Darling was Jack's partner and also Cassie's husband. Cassie waved to Jack from behind the counter, where she was rearranging the muffins on the muffin rack. "Hi, Jack! Give John a kiss for me."

Jack smiled. "I think I'll let you do that. Wouldn't want to give him ideas."

Nans spun around in her seat to face Jack. "It's so great to see you, Jack. I hardly ever see you anymore. And you haven't asked us to consult on any cases."

Jack put the lid on one paper cup and then started filling the second. "I miss you too, Mona. Maybe you should have us for dinner."

Nans turned back to the table and fluffed a napkin in her lap. "Speaking of dinner, I do have a batch of homemade ravioli in my fridge for you, which I'd be willing to trade for a consultant gig or maybe some information on the Maguire case."

"Ravioli? Cheese, mushroom, or spinach?" Jack asked. Nans's homemade ravioli were one of Jack's favorite meals.

"Cheese. Just the way you like them."

Jack placed the lid on the second cup and came to stand next to their table. "We don't really have a need to hire on consultants right now, but I did discover something interesting about the Maguire case that I can share."

Nans's brows shot up. "Do tell."

"Have you considered that Henry Maguire might actually be the killer?" Jack asked.

"Of course. That is one of the possibilities we are investigating," Nans said. "But don't you agree that evidence is flimsy? And Muriel said he was such a good boy."

Jack gave her an indulgent smile. "Grandmas always think their grandsons are good, so I don't think we can really take that into account officially."

"I guess not." Nans bit into the Cup and Cake lemon square. Lexy noticed that Ida had managed to devour the one they'd brought from the Confection Connection and was now wrapping part of her brownie in a napkin.

"What makes you think he did it?" Lexy asked. "You sound like you have new information that might render the evidence we know about not so flimsy."

Jack signed. "Well, I'm not aware of all the evidence since our department didn't investigate, so I can't say if it's flimsy or not. I did put some feelers out, and Henry's alibi is definitely sketchy. There's no one to corroborate that he was driving around after he left the hospital, and he would have had just enough time to rush home and murder his wife."

Nans made a face. "That doesn't sound like enough to convict him."

"Of course it isn't. I'm sure they have more over at the New Ipswich police department, or they wouldn't have arrested him. I'm trying to get more information on the case without ruffling any feathers, but just keep in mind that Henry might not be the good little boy that Muriel thinks he is. Seems he was picked up on a loitering charge a few months back."

"Loitering? Where?" Lexy asked.

"Under the bridge by the train track. It's policed pretty heavily since vagrants and drug users are known to hang out there," Jack said.

"Hmmm… well, that does complicate things." Nans chewed a bite of her molasses cookie thoughtfully.

"There might be more. I've got my feelers out, but for now I think you should proceed with caution." Jack looked down at Lexy.

"We always do." Lexy smiled up at him.

Jack nodded and started toward the door. "At least if Henry is the killer, he's no threat to you locked up behind bars."

Once Jack was out the door and safely out of earshot, Nans looked at them over the rim of her coffee mug. "And if he's not the killer and someone wants the police to keep thinking that he is, then that person could be a very dangerous threat indeed."

CHAPTER 8

"Come on up and I'll give you those homemade ravioli for Jack," Nans said as Lexy dropped them off at the Brook Ridge Falls Retirement Center later that afternoon. Lexy didn't really have a lot of time to linger, as she had a lot of work to catch up on back at the Cup and Cake, but she supposed it wouldn't hurt to run up and grab the ravioli. Besides, it would make Jack happy, and when Jack was happy, Lexy was happy.

"I'm not convinced Henry is the killer," Helen said as she inspected the signs on the lawn to make sure Mario didn't mess with them. "You ask me, Mario is behind this."

Ruth tsked. "Let's not jump to conclusions."

Helen turned to her. "Don't tell me you have a crush on him. He's nasty."

Ruth rankled. "Just because he's your competition, doesn't make him a killer. What would his motive be?"

"Ladies!" Nans stood with her hands on her hips. "We're not very far into the case. We have nothing conclusive so far, so let's not make assumptions."

"Uh oh…" Ida's eyes were on something behind Lexy. Lexy turned to see Mario and Endora coming up the sidewalk.

Helen's eyes narrowed on Mario. "If he wants a fight, I'll give him a fight."

Nans held her hand out in front of Helen. "Now, hold on. He's probably just walking up the sidewalk."

Mario stopped in front of them, glaring first at Nans then at Helen. "Just what, exactly, are you people up to?"

"What do you mean? We're going into the building." Ida stepped up to Mario and straightened as if to try to make herself taller. She was just a tad over five feet, so it didn't really accomplish much. "It's a public sidewalk."

"Not that," Endora said in her grating voice. "We saw you at the Confection Connection. You're following us."

"Following *you*? You're following *me*! Trying to undermine me in the election. Moving my signs." Helen gestured to the signs on the lawn. "And spying on me!"

"This isn't about the election. This is about my Rosie. You're trying to get that weasel off that killed her." Mario pointed a gnarled finger at Nans. "I heard you talking to Muriel Maguire. That boy is a killer and should serve time."

"Really? Then what were *you* doing at the bakery?"

"We weren't at the bakery. We were just in town, shopping," Endora said.

Would Mario's presence there necessarily indicate that he was guilty of killing his own granddaughter? She had to admit that Helen might be a little biased in her rivalry with Mario for the president's position.

"Just why are you so concerned about us investigating? Got something to hide?" Ida asked.

"Hide? No." Mario's eyes misted, and a pang of sympathy pierced Lexy's heart. "Rosa was a good girl. A talented trapeze artist. She had everything to live for and was cut down in the prime of her life. That's why I'm concerned. I want justice for my granddaughter."

"But what if Henry didn't kill her? What if the

police were wrong? Were they having marital trouble?" Nans asked.

Mario frowned. "I don't know about any trouble. But if Henry didn't kill her, then who did?" He shoved past them, pulling Endora in his wake.

"That's what we plan to find out," Ida called after him before opening the door and gesturing for the rest of them to precede her inside.

The Brook Ridge Falls Retirement Center had a big lobby with overstuffed chairs and couches that acted like a social area where residents could gather. There were tables with games and a big-screen tv. Several residents were milling about, and Helen made a beeline for them, turning on her campaign-trail charm.

She shook hands with everyone, reminding them about her campaign promise for the Saturday coffee socials and to vote for her at the election on Friday.

Nans did her best to hurry Helen along, and when she finally broke free, they rushed to the stairway.

They were halfway across the lobby when Lexy heard "Psst... Mona!"

They turned to see Muriel Maguire standing next to a large potted palm. She was casting furtive glances out the large glass windows in front. "I saw you being accosted by Mario… was he telling you some lies about Henry?"

Nans shook her head. "No. He does seem to think Henry killed Rosa though."

Muriel crossed her arms over her chest. "He would. Or maybe he's trying to cover for one of his own family." She lowered her voice. "I was just wondering if you'd discovered anything that can clear Henry yet."

"Not yet. But we did discover something that is a bit concerning," Nans said.

Muriel's brows knit together. "What?"

"Henry had some trouble with the police before."

Muriel shifted her weight and glanced down at her feet. "That has nothing to do with Rosa's murder. And besides, it wasn't the big scandal you think it was!"

Ida rummaged in her purse, pulled out a napkin-wrapped cookie, and broke a piece off. "Scandal? I'd hardly call loitering a scandal."

Muriel looked surprised. "Loitering? Oh, right. That's not really a scandal…" She glanced over at the TV. "Oh, look! Wheel of Fortune is on. Gotta go!"

Muriel practically ran to the TV, and Helen turned to Nans. "What odd behavior. What do you think that was all about?"

Nans shook her head slowly, her eyes tracking Muriel as she sat down on the blue sofa in the corner. "I have no idea, but I know one thing. Henry is starting to look a bit more suspicious, don't you think?"

*L*exy only stayed long enough to pick up the ravioli and watch Nans write the new clues up on the whiteboard. Then she rushed over to the Cup and Cake to help Cassie out with the baking. She was late getting home but was armed with Nans's ravioli and a Boston cream pie, so she figured Jack wouldn't complain.

Sprinkles met her at the door with her usual exuberant greeting. Lexy put down the cake box long enough to pick Sprinkles up for a hug. She then gently placed her down and proceeded to the kitchen, Sprinkles's nails clicking on the polished hardwood floors as she passed through the living room.

The old-fashioned Formica table—a hand-me-down from Nans—was set, and a teal bowl filled with lush green lettuce and bright-red tomatoes sat in the middle. Jack was at the stove, stirring a simmering pot of tomato sauce with a wooden spoon.

Jack's eyes lit up when he saw the ravioli. He reached out for the bag. "I've been waiting for you."

Judging by the way his eyes were glued to the ziplock bag, Lexy couldn't really tell if he was talking to her or the golden-white pillows of pasta nestled inside it. "Are you talking to me or the pasta?"

Jack's eyes shifted from the bag to Lexy. "You, of course." He gave her a brief kiss and took the bag and the bakery box. "What's in the box?"

"Boston cream pie."

"Excellent." Jack put the bakery box in the fridge then started loading the ravioli into a pot of boiling water, spooning them out with care so they didn't break. "Just a few minutes and we'll be ready to eat."

"What can I do?" Lexy asked, already looking in the fridge for the wine.

"Wine is a great idea," Jack said. "And there's garlic bread in the oven. Should be just about ready."

Lexy pulled the garlic bread out and put it in a basket then poured two glasses of wine while Jack finished up the pasta.

They sat across from each other at the table.

Sprinkles sat on the floor between them, her gaze fixated on every bite they took.

Lexy savored a bite of ravioli with its creamy ricotta cheese filling and tangy marinara sauce. "So, how was your day?"

"Great. After I left the Cup and Cake, I went back to the office and did some paperwork. Not too much going on in the crime department in Brook Ridge Falls these days."

Lexy forked up another bite of ravioli. "Does that mean you had time to look into the case against Henry?"

Jack slipped Sprinkles a piece of lettuce. "I did. Unfortunately, I can't dig too deep because I don't want to set off warning bells for the detectives in New Ipswich. Professional courtesy dictates that we stay out of each other's cases unless we have a new lead or suspect something is amiss. And quite honestly, I don't think anything is amiss. It seems that Henry isn't the innocent little boy that his grandmother thinks he is."

Lexy remembered how Muriel had let something about a scandal slip. Maybe Muriel didn't think he was all that innocent, though, because she'd acted very cagey after the slip-up, as if she were covering for Henry. "Turns out she might not think he's that innocent."

Jack's left brow quirked up. "Oh?"

Lexy tore off a piece of garlic bread. "She sought us out when I dropped the ladies off at the retirement center this afternoon. She wanted an update on the case, but while we were talking, she let it slip that Henry was involved in some sort of scandal."

"What sort of scandal?"

Lexy shrugged. "I don't know. She clammed up after that. Though she did mention something about it not being what people thought it was. I think she might be blind to Henry's faults."

Jack's eyes narrowed as he sipped his wine. "Interesting. The scandal might have something to do with what I found out about Henry today."

"What did you find?" Lexy bit into the bread. It was crunchy on the surface and soft on the inside and infused with the tangy-sweet combination of garlic and butter.

"Turns out one of their neighbors called the police on him a few times because he was consorting with unsavory characters."

"Unsavory characters? What does that mean?"

"I'm not sure, but it sounds like the neighbor didn't like the people they saw hanging around

Henry's apartment, and *that*, combined with the loitering under the bridge… well… it all might lead one to assume that Henry was up to something shady… scandalous even."

Lexy nodded. "It would, wouldn't it? What was the name of the neighbor that complained?"

Jack reached for a piece of bread. "Sorry. The name was redacted from the police file. A lot of people ask not to be identified."

Lexy bit into another piece of garlic bread. It was looking more and more like Muriel was wrong about Henry. And now, they had this unsavory character lead. They needed to know more about that, but in order to find out more, they'd have to find out who the complaining neighbor was. And if anyone could figure out how to get that information, it would be Nans.

CHAPTER 10

The next morning, Lexy got to the bakery early and knocked off a lot of her chores then left Cassie to mind the store while she headed to Nans with a bakery box full of pastry. She'd called ahead and told Nans that Jack had given her an important clue about the case. She couldn't wait to tell them.

Nans was waiting at the door when she arrived. Ida took the bakery box and hurried to fill the pastry plate on the table. Today, she'd brought cheese Danish, oatmeal cookies, and lemon-poppyseed muffins.

Nans had coffee ready, and Lexy took her place across from Ruth at the dining room table. The seat next to Ruth, usually occupied by Helen, was empty.

"Where's Helen?" Lexy asked as she spread some butter on a muffin.

"She's coming. I guess she had some business concerning the election to take care of first." Nans poured a second cup of coffee, the dark liquid settling into her dainty china cup like mud.

"I sure hope she wins the election, or we'll be hearing about it for months," Ruth said.

"I heard her say she might ask for a recount if Mario wins." Ida munched on a Danish. "She said she wouldn't put it past him to engage in election tampering."

Ruth frowned. "Don't you think that's a little over the top? I mean, this is only an election for the president of the community center. There's no real power in that."

Nans snorted. "Don't tell Helen that."

Ruth laughed. "I wouldn't dare."

Nans uncapped the pen, letting the noxious smell waft out. "Lexy, you've kept us in suspense long enough. What is this big news?"

Lexy was eager to tell them, but it felt weird to start discussing it without Helen. "Should we wait for Helen?"

Nans looked at her watch. "It's twenty of ten. She was supposed to be here ten minutes ago. She knows we're on a tight schedule, so I say we go ahead without her."

"Yeah, you snooze, you lose," Ida said.

Lexy suppressed a smile. The ladies were all business when it came to discussing a case, but the truth was they really didn't have a schedule. They were all retired with nothing much else to do except go to yoga, bingo, and watch Wheel of Fortune. But if it made them feel more useful to run the case on a schedule, then she supposed that was okay with her. "Okay then. Jack hasn't been able to get a lot of information. He doesn't want to dig too deep and get in trouble with the detectives investigating the case."

"Yeah, we know that." Ida picked a muffin from the pastry tray.

Lexy took a sip of coffee, which pretty much tasted the way it had looked—dark, thick, and strong. Nans must have needed some extra oomph this morning. She put the cup aside and continued. "Jack isn't convinced that Henry is innocent. There was that report where Henry was arrested for loitering at the bridge, and Jack came across an official complaint from one of Henry's neighbors about unsavory characters hanging around Henry's apartment."

Ida looked excited. "Unsavory characters? That sounds like fun. What was unsavory about them?"

Lexy shrugged. "I don't know. Jack couldn't get descriptions or anything."

Nans wrote this down on the whiteboard. "We'll have to get those ourselves by talking to the neighbor. This could be the big break we need. What was the neighbor's name?"

Lexy brushed muffin crumbs from her hand onto the napkin. "Unfortunately, I couldn't find that out. Jack said they omit the names from the official report if the complainant asks to be left out."

Nans turned to face them, her lips pressed together. "Huh. I guess we'll have to figure out who that was ourselves."

"Too bad Ruth can't use her flirty methods for getting information out of the cops like she used to when she was young," Ida teased.

"I never flirted with cops for information!" Ruth acted shocked, but Lexy could see that underneath, she was secretly pleased that Ida had remembered.

"We won't be able to find out from the cops. We don't have an 'in' at the police department in New Ipswich like we do here." Nans nodded at Lexy. "We're going to have to find out who it was another way."

"Why don't we just ask Henry?" Ida said.

Nans nodded and pointed the marker at Ida. "Now *that* is smart thinking."

"But he's in jail. How will we get in?" Lexy remembered her promise to Jack. She couldn't break that promise, and besides, one couldn't just waltz into the prison and ask to meet with an inmate.

"Good point." Nans pointed her marker at Ruth. "Ruth, do you have any connections that can get us in?"

Ruth scowled at Nans over the rim of her coffee cup. "Who do you think I am? Whitey Bulger? I don't have those kinds of connections."

"I can't go anyway," Lexy said. "I promised Jack I wouldn't go to the prison to visit any inmates."

Nans frowned. "Now why would you make a silly promise like that?"

"It was the only way he would look into the case."

Ida slurped her coffee. "Mona, this stuff tastes like mud." She turned to Lexy. "What *exactly* did you promise?"

Lexy thought back to the conversation with Jack. "I think I specifically promised that I wouldn't go to the prison to talk to any inmates."

"Ha! Then I have an idea!" Ida pushed up from the table and went to the row of bookcases in Nans's living room. She picked out an old hardcover and held it up. "Remember how we saw Vinny wheeling the library cart around?"

They all nodded.

"What if we donate some books to the prison library?" Ida waved a hand in front of the bookcases, which were filled to the brim. "That might get us inside, and then maybe we can find a way to talk to Henry. Muriel said he got to sit in the common room there and teach the inmates chess because he was on good behavior. We might get lucky."

"That could work," Nans said. "And the prison is near one of the bakeries on our list. Doughy Delights. We could stop by there afterwards."

"I hope they have a better product than the last bakery." Ruth glanced at Lexy. "Though of course, no bakery could be as good as Lexy's"

"Lexy can come with us and see for herself." Ida started to pull books off the shelves.

"I wish. I promised Jack I wouldn't go to the prison, though," Lexy said.

"You promised him that you wouldn't go to the prison *to talk to inmates*." Ida stacked some of the books on Nans's glass coffee table. "But what about going to the prison to donate books? That's entirely different. It's an act of charity. And if we happen to run into an inmate and talk to them… well then, that won't really be breaking your promise, would it?"

Lexy sipped her mud and thought about that. She supposed it technically wasn't breaking her promise. But if she joined them in the prison and Jack found out… would he see it that way too?

CHAPTER 11

*H*elen was coming down the hallway as they left Nans's apartment.

"Glad you could make it, Helen," Ida said sarcastically.

"Sorry, but you won't believe why I was late!" Helen huffed. "I caught Mario Blondini looking in my windows. I knew he was spying on me. Probably trying to get a leg up on the election. Well, two can play at that game. Come on!"

Helen did an about-face and headed back toward the stairs. Lexy, Ida, Ruth, and Nans did double-time to catch up.

"How would spying on you help in the election?" Ida asked.

"Who knows. But I'm going to show him he can't

mess with me. Blondini lives in one of those single-family homes on Oak Street, right around the corner, and I'm going to show him that he's not the only one that can spy." Helen glanced at the grocery bag loaded with books that Ruth was struggling along with. "What's that?"

They told her about their plan to visit the jail on the pretext of donating books. Helen nodded approvingly. "Good. I did some more research on that Broadmoore heist. Remember that Cassie heard the Circo Acrobata might have been involved in it? I have a suspicion."

"Oh? What?" Lexy asked.

"I think Rosa might have been involved. But I need to talk to Vinny first." Helen turned down Oak Street, full speed ahead.

"If she was, that could shed new light on why she was murdered," Nans said.

"Shhh... this is his place here." Helen stopped in front of a nice brick Colonial-style home located in the single-family dwelling section of the retirement village.

"Okay. Let's sneak around the side." Helen pushed her way through a shrubbery, and the rest followed, disregarding that it was broad daylight and anyone could see them. Helen appeared determined to be sneaky, crouching down low and scurrying over to the corner of the house then flattening herself against the warm bricks as she made her way to the back.

In back, she stopped in front of a large bay window. Standing on tiptoes, her nose was even with the bottom of it. They all peered in.

"Looks like he rushed out. I hope he doesn't think he's going to crash the book club meeting. That's where I was campaigning this morning." Helen glanced at her watch. "I didn't see him there, and it's over now, so if that's what he was up to, he's too late!"

It was a dining room, the long table set as if ready for brunch. The room was decorated lavishly with a crystal chandelier, rich dark-colored walls, and heavily carved antique furniture. Gorgeous vases loaded with flowers stood on several sideboards and in the middle of the table.

A large grandfather clock in the corner chimed, making them all jump. Ten o'clock. Luckily, the house appeared empty. The last thing Lexy wanted was to have the police summoned and have Jack arrest her for being a Peeping Tom!

On the table, gold linen napkins sat next to settings of fine china. Cut crystal glasses sparkled near sterling silver flatware.

The sideboard was filled with serving dishes. A three-tiered platter held pastries. Lexy squinted to get a better look. Had those come from her bakery? She spied the bakery box on the hardwood floor beside the server. Not hers—hers had a pink cup on the top, and this one had a blue bee. "I guess they don't have good taste. The baked goods came from another bakery."

"Shameful." Ida shook her head.

"I don't see anything shady in there," Nans said to Helen.

"Look closer. There's got to be something," Helen said. "Look at all the stuff he has. Is that real gold? And what about that china? It looks like those Limoges could be worth a lot."

"So? None of this means he is doing something shady with the election," Ruth said.

Helen glared at her. "He is. You saw him move my signs. You're just making excuses because you have a—"

Thwack!

A knife quivered in the window trim right next to Helen's head, and they turned to see Rosa's cousin glaring at them with flat dark eyes.

"You people are trespassing."

Ida fisted her hands on her hips. "Who are you?"

"William Blondini. This is my uncle's place." His

gaze shifted to Helen, his eyes narrowing. "I know who you are. You're the lady running against my uncle. What are you doing peeking in his windows?"

"We weren't peeking in any windows." Ruth held up the bag of books in her hand. "We were dropping off a book."

"A book?" William didn't look convinced. "Then why are you skulking out back?"

"We usually drop them off on the back porch. It's a thing." Ruth plucked a book out of the bag and trotted over to the deck, putting the book onto a chair. She turned and looked at William. "See?"

"I think you were spying." William reached past Helen, causing her to shrink back. He pulled the knife out of the wood, looking at the blade as it glinted in the light. Helen scuttled away from him.

He gave her a sinister smile. "Don't worry… if I wanted to hit you, I would have. I have perfect aim, you know."

"That's very nice," Nans said. "I bet that comes in handy with the circus show. Now, we've delivered the book and must be on our way." She started off toward the street.

"Toodles," Ida said, falling in step behind Nans.

"Nice meeting you." Ruth hurried past him to catch up with Nans.

Lexy pushed Helen in front of her and brought up the rear.

"You ladies better be careful. Leave my uncle alone. And mind your own business if you know what's good for you. I'll be watching."

Lexy looked over her shoulder at William, who was flicking the knife back and forth in his hands. She suppressed a shudder and hurried to the street. Suddenly, the visit to the jail and talking to felons seemed mild compared to a knife-throwing Blondini.

*L*exy hemmed and hawed about actually going into the prison, but in the end, the ladies' advice about how they were simply donating books won out. The clincher was when Ruth shoved the bag of books into Lexy's hand and claimed it was too heavy for any of them to carry, so if Jack found out, she could simply say she was just saving them from ruining their backs. Lexy felt a little guilty about it, but she also wanted to hear what Henry had to say for herself, *if* they even got a chance to talk to him.

Inside the lobby, Nans marched up to the guard in the reception area. "We're from the Ladies Auxiliary with the book donation."

The guard, a white-haired man who looked like he was more interested in retiring than processing visitors, gave her a confused look. "Book donation? What's that about?"

Lexy opened the bag and tipped it toward him so he could see inside.

"It's a new program. We're supposed to deliver them. You need books for the library, don't you?" Nans asked.

His expression turned dubious. "I don't know anything about a book donation."

"Well, I don't think Greta down at the town hall will be happy about that," Ruth huffed. "You know how she hates it when someone drops the ball." Ruth looked pointedly at the guard. "And someone has surely dropped the ball here."

Ruth seemed to have contacts everywhere, and apparently, Greta was one of them. Lexy wasn't sure who Greta was, but the guard certainly did. Just the mention of her name had instilled a look of fear in his eye.

"This is one of Greta's programs?" he asked.

Ruth whipped out her phone. "It sure is. Let me call her and find out what the problem is. What did you say your name is?"

The guard stood. "No need to call. We can always use books. I'll just have Jimmy escort you."

Ruth smiled and tucked her phone back into her

large purse as the guard pressed the buzzer and the door clicked open.

Jimmy met them on the other side of the door. He had short cropped hair and was wearing a starched green uniform. He looked to be in his mid-thirties, and his demeanor was quite serious.

"Take them to the library and wait to escort them back," the desk guard instructed.

Jimmy nodded at him. "Follow me." He spun around and started down the hall.

They were silent as they followed him to the common area adjacent to the library. Jimmy opened the door and gestured for them to go inside. Then he took up his station next to the door, and Lexy and the ladies headed toward the small room where the books were kept.

The area itself wasn't much to write home about. It was utilitarian with long tables and plastic chairs. There were no windows, but the overhead lighting was bright. The flooring was the same green and gray tile as the lobby. Lexy supposed it was better than sitting in a jail cell. One inmate was sitting at a desk using a computer. Another was reading in a chair. The good news was that Henry sat in front of a chess set at a small table in the corner.

"Ruth! I guess you must have missed me!" Vinny came through the door, wheeling the library cart.

"Hi, Vinny. We brought some books to donate to the library." Ruth gestured toward Lexy's bag.

Vinny looked inside the bag. "That's great. Looks like some good ones in there. Come into the office, and I'll log them in."

They followed him to a small room in the corner and squeezed inside. The room was neat as a pin. Apparently, there was no clutter in prison. An old computer sat on a desk, and Vinny sat down in front of it. He slipped on a pair of half-moon reading glasses and typed a few keys. The screen went wonky, and he gave it a whack, returning it to normal.

He grabbed a book from the bag. "Now, let me see. Oh! No Scone Unturned by Leighann Dobbs. That's one of my favorites."

He pecked at the keys with two fingers, taking a full five minutes to put in just the title. Ida fidgeted. Nans sighed. Helen glanced out into the other room as if looking for potential voters.

Ruth cleared her throat. "Say, Vinny, I was wondering about that heist. The one that put you in here."

Vinny scowled over his reading glasses at her. "Yeah. That was a bum deal."

"I heard that it was quite a mystery how you got inside," Ruth said.

Vinny smiled. "Yeah, it was clever. No regular robbers could have pulled that off. See, they had an alarm system with laser beams, and you had to have a lot of skills to duck under and over. Would be impossible for most people."

Ruth leaned her hip against the desk and lowered her voice. "But not for an acrobat."

Vinny glanced over his shoulder. "Hey, I didn't say that…"

"Oh, I know," Ruth made light of it. "But let's say it did take a lot of gymnastics. An acrobat would be perfect. And if there was a whole family of them, well… one of them could be the one who ratted you out."

Vinny's eyebrows mashed together. "Yeah. The rat. I'd like to find that person. But *if* there were some acrobats involved." He raised his brows at Ruth. "And I'm not saying there was. It wasn't just about being able to do cartwheels. Someone had to plan out the whole thing. There was a mastermind behind the whole thing and that wasn't necessarily someone out in the field."

Ruth raised her brows and looked out the doorway. Lexy turned to follow her gaze. It went straight to Henry Maguire.

"Would that person have to know different strategies and be a big thinker?" Ruth asked.

"Yeah, I'll say." Vinny started pecking at the keyboard again. "Because it wouldn't be easy to figure out the timing. You'd need a precise strategy."

"Uh huh." Ruth nodded at Nans and the ladies. "Well, I hope you enjoy the books. Nice seeing you." She pushed away from the desk and headed out into the adjoining room.

"Thanks for the books, ladies! Come back any time!" Vinny yelled as they made a beeline for Henry Maguire.

Henry looked up at their approach. His eyes sparked with recognition then became guarded. Did Henry have something to hide?

"Is something wrong with my grandmother?" Henry asked.

"Oh no, dear. We were donating some books and saw you here and thought we'd say hello. Isn't that right, girls?" Nans turned to Lexy and the ladies, and they all nodded.

Henry let out a breath and relaxed back into the chair. "Oh, good. I knew you were friends with her since you came the other day and was afraid it was bad news when I saw you coming toward me without her."

"Nothing of the sort," Helen said. "She's fit as a fiddle."

"Muriel tells us you're teaching some of the inmates how to play chess." Ruth gestured toward the chess board. "You must spend a lot of time playing and thinking up strategy."

Henry fiddled with the chess piece he was holding in his hand—the king, Lexy assumed, by the size and crown on the top. "You could say that."

"You must be very smart," Ida said.

"My grandmother thinks so." Henry tapped the chess piece on the table.

"Yeah, knowing all those moves. Like which one goes forward and when to move them back," Helen said.

"And which ones go diagonal," Ruth added.

"What about the one that goes up two spaces and across one?" Ida frowned down at the board. "That one always confuses me."

"It's not that hard. I could teach you sometime—if I ever get out of here, that is." Henry stopped fiddling with the king. "Have you guys found anything out about my case? Gram told me you were looking into it."

Nans shuffled on her feet. "We're looking into a few things. But it would help us out if you could answer a question."

"Okay." Henry drew out the word as if he were hesitant.

"A neighbor complained about you. I was wondering if you knew who that was."

Henry made a face. "Yeah, I know who it was. The old busybody in the apartment across the hall. Doris Pettigrew. She was wrong though. I never had anyone come to visit except other doctors."

"Are you sure?" Nans asked.

Henry started fiddling with the king again. "Yes, I'm sure."

"Well, what about this scandal we heard about?" Ida's question earned a sharp look from Nans. Apparently, Nans had been getting around to that in her own time, and Ida had jumped the gun.

Henry's eyes shuttered, and he glanced toward the guard at the door. "Scandal? I don't know what you are talking about."

"We're sure it's nothing…" Nans tried to prompt him into explaining.

"Ladies! Are you done with the books?" The guard was coming toward them from his position at the door. "No loitering here."

"Right, okay."

"No problem."

"I guess so. Nice talking to you Henry."

Henry went back to his chess game without giving them so much as a glance as they left.

CHAPTER 13

*D*oughy Delights was on the way home from the prison, so naturally, they headed there right away. The bakery was in an old mill building and featured antique oak bakery cases and creaky, wide pine flooring. Lexy supposed it was cute in a vintage sort of way. It had a coffee station and steel-and-oak tables with an industrial look. The smell of coffee and cookies permeated the air. Ida took a deep whiff and rushed to the bakery case.

"At least these products are bigger than the Confection Connection." Ida crouched down, pressing her face to the glass to get a good look at the bottom row.

"Yeah, but let's see how they taste." Helen winked at Lexy.

"Ladies, are you forgetting why we're here?" Nans gestured toward another case, where rows of muffins were lined up waiting to be purchased. Bran muffins, blueberry, lemon-poppyseed and, yes, corn muffins all stood in straight rows. The corn muffins did not have sugar crystals on them.

Nans moved over to the counter, and a baker in a white chef's coat appeared from the back. "Can I help you?"

Nans nodded toward the muffin case. "Your corn muffins look lovely, but do you have any with sugar crystals on top?"

The baker shook his head and looked at Nans as if she needed to be educated. "No, ma'am, corn muffins are too textured already. Sugar crystals on top would create a bad experience for the palate."

"I see. So you never sell them like that?"

"Certainly not. If you like sugar crystals on top, try the blueberry. They are much more delicate and refined. The added sweetness makes them pop!" He accentuated the word "pop" with a flourish of his hand.

"Okay. I guess I'll take one of those," Nans said. "You don't happen to know of another bakery that sells them with sugar crystals on top?"

The baker stopped mid-package and looked up at

Nans. "Another bakery? No, I do not go into other bakeries scouting out their wares."

Lexy cringed and tried not to blush. She wasn't exactly scouting out the wares. They were on an investigation, but she still felt guilty. Though there was nothing wrong with scoping out the competition—big companies did it all the time.

The ladies completed their orders: Ida with a cinnamon scone, Helen a strawberry muffin, Ruth a hermit, and Lexy a giant elephant ear that looked incredibly flaky and sweet with a tiny sprinkling of cinnamon.

"I'll help you eat that if you can't finish it," Ida said as they took their purchases to one of the tables.

"I think I might need some help." Lexy was serious—the thing was as big as both her hands put together.

Lexy got settled in her seat and broke off half of the flaky pastry then passed it to Ida.

Ida bit in and made yum-yum noises. The yum-yum noises were appropriate, Lexy discovered, as she dug into hers. It was flaky but not dry, and the sugar and cinnamon made her taste buds dance.

"So, looks like we struck out again," Ruth said.

"Yeah. But we hit pay dirt with Henry." Nans bit into her muffin. "Hmmm, this isn't bad."

"This hermit is pretty good, too," Ruth said then quickly added, "Not as good as yours, Lexy."

"Thanks." Lexy broke off another piece of elephant ear. She had to admit this bakery wasn't too bad. The pastries were very good, and it had ambiance. No sparkling waterfall across the street like the Cup and Cake, but it was still pleasant. "It sure seemed like Henry was hiding something. He clammed up as soon as you mentioned the scandal, and I think he lied about the neighbor's complaint."

"What makes you say he lied?" Helen, who had cut her muffin in half then slathered a full pat of butter onto each side, asked.

"He said the only people that came to visit him were doctors. Surely, the neighbor wouldn't think they were unsavory," Lexy said.

"Maybe or maybe not. And we aren't sure the visitors were for him, either." Nans sipped her coffee.

"You mean they could have been visiting the wife?" Ida spread a napkin out in front of her and plunked her cinnamon scone in the middle then wrapped it up and shoved it in her purse.

Nans nodded. "Yes. And maybe that is a clue to the identity of her killer."

"Or maybe Henry is the killer, and that's why he's lying," Ida said.

"Could be," Nans replied.

"Or maybe Mario or one of his crew is the killer." Helen took the last bite of her hermit.

"You really are after him, aren't you?" Ruth asked. "Just because he's running against you is no reason to malign the man."

"It's not that. I think her murder might have something to do with the Broadmoore heist. Vinny admitted acrobats were involved, and the Blondinis are part of the Circo Acrobata. One of them has already ratted out Vinny. Maybe Rosa was the rat and was planning on ratting out more people and got killed for it."

"Or maybe Rosa knew who the rat was and that's why she was killed."

Ruth shook her head. "I think you are jumping to conclusions. None of this implicates Mario."

Helen balled up her napkin and shoved it in her empty paper coffee cup. "It seems quite obvious to me!"

Nans pushed up from the table. "Ladies, no fighting. We have more clues to collect before we can start making assumptions."

"And let's not forget Henry." Lexy remembered how fidgety he was with those chess pieces. "He could be involved. Plus, he benefitted from her life insurance."

"Oh, I haven't crossed him off my list. But we must investigate all angles," Nans said. "Speaking of which… Lexy, do you have time to drive over to Henry's apartment building? Doris Pettigrew should be easy to find. Henry said she lived right across the hall."

CHAPTER 14

"So, this is the scene of the crime," Ida said as they pulled up in front of an old Victorian. From outward appearances, it was hard to imagine that something sinister had happened inside. It was nicely kept, with off-white siding and purple trim.

"Looks like a birthday cake," Ruth said as they walked up the steps toward the purple door. She opened the door to reveal a small entryway. A set of stairs loomed in front of them. Old-fashioned green flowered wallpaper papered the walls. The floor was hardwood, scuffed from years of wear. To the right was a solid oak door with the number Two on it.

"According to the case files, Rosa and Henry lived at number two." Nans gestured toward the door on the other side of the hall which had a number One. "So this one must be Mrs. Pettigrew."

Ruth was standing closest to the door, so she knocked.

"Who is it?" A voice drifted out almost before the knock stopped echoing. Clearly, Mrs. Pettigrew kept a close eye on the place and had seen them come in.

"It's the Ladies' Detective Agency." Nans's voice took on an official tone. "We have some questions on a case if you'd be so kind as to answer them."

Of course, Doris Pettigrew would be thrilled to answer questions. If she was truly the busybody that it sounded like she was, she wouldn't be able to resist the lure of gossip and finding out exactly what case the ladies were referring to.

Lexy heard a series of locks clicking and chains sliding, and then the door cracked and a rheumy blue eye appeared. "Do you have any credentials?"

"Of course." Nans shoved a business card at her. It was in a laminate case, so it resembled an official badge of some sort.

Doris snatched the card and pulled it inside. It took her a few seconds, but Nans's card must have passed muster because the door opened and Doris said, "Come in."

Ida went in first. "Oh, this is… unusual."

Lexy peered over Ida's head. She couldn't be sure exactly what Ida thought was unusual. There were so many things. It could have been the giant four-foot-tall dolls that stood around the edge of the room. Or it might have been the knitted afghans that covered every surface. Or maybe it was the stuffed animals that were sitting on the couch as if holding a conversation. Then again, it might have been the herd of cats that was sniffing around Ida's ankles.

Doris handed the card back to Nans. "I'm Doris Pettigrew, by the way."

They all introduced themselves, and Doris gestured toward the living room for them to sit.

Ida gingerly plucked a large pink elephant off the sofa and put it on the floor then took its place. A black cat immediately jumped into her lap. The rest of the ladies followed her lead, moving dolls aside, disturbing stuffed animals, and pushing cats out of their laps.

Lexy sat in the only chair not occupied by a stuffed animal. The smell of mothballs wafted up as the rough wool of the crocheted granny square pillow irritated her arm.

Achoo! Helen sneezed and pushed the fluffy tail of a white Persian out of her face.

"God bless you." Doris handed her a tissue.

"Now, let's get to the point. I know why you are here."

"You do?" Nans petted the tiger cat that had settled into her lap. It was a tiny little thing with a white face and paws. Lexy could hear it purring from where she sat.

Doris nodded. "It's about that killer across the hall, isn't it? I told the police he was no good. They didn't listen."

Ruth rolled her eyes. "Yeah, we know how that can be."

Achoo! Helen sneezed in agreement, and Doris handed her another tissue.

"We heard that you filed a complaint." Nans bent down to pet the ginger striped cat that was rubbing its cheek on her ankle.

"Yeah, and if they'd done something, that nice girl might still be alive." Doris shook her head and tutted. "Such a shame."

"Rosa? You knew her well?" Nans asked

"No. Not *well*. But she seemed nice. She would say hello in the morning and even helped me catch Bartholomew once when he escaped." Doris smiled indulgently at a large black-and-white tuxedo cat lounging on top of a doily-covered mahogany credenza. "Didn't she, you naughty kitty."

Bartholomew blinked lazily, his green eyes glaring at them.

Nans shifted in her seat and patted beside her for the orange cat to jump up. "What about Henry? Did you know him well?"

Doris made a face. "He wasn't as nice. Actually, I guess I never really saw him that much."

"But you saw people coming to visit him that scared you," Ida said.

"Yes. Some very suspicious characters came to visit. An old lady living alone can't be too careful these days," Doris said.

"Of course not," Nans agreed.

Achoo! Ruth nodded.

"So did these people come often?" Nans asked.

Doris pressed her lips together and thought about that for a minute. "One lady did. And I'm using the term *lady* very loosely."

Ida leaned forward, and the cat jumped out of her lap. "Can you describe her?"

Doris shuddered. "She was most unsavory looking. Young. Dark hair. But the disturbing thing about her appearance was the snake tattoo on her arm."

Ida's eyes grew wide. "Snake tattoo?"

"Yes, it was big and went all around here." Doris gestured toward her bicep, around her arm, and down to her wrist. "It was garish, all black and red and green with gold eyes, and its forked tongue was sticking out! Very realistic."

"Blech." Ruth pulled the cat in her lap closer.

"Did you see this woman with Henry?" Nans asked.

Doris squinted her eyes as if trying to picture if she'd seen Henry and the tattoo lady. "I'm not sure if I actually saw them together, but I saw her at their door plenty of times. I have no idea why Henry would take up with her when he had Rosa. She was so beautiful and so nice."

"You mentioned that." Helen glanced at her watch. Lexy imagined she was probably anxious to get back to her campaigning. There was only one day left for her to add to her voter count before the election.

"It seems like you are very observant," Nans said.

"Why, thank you." Doris shifted in her seat, beaming with pride.

"So, the night Rosa died, you must have seen or heard something." Nans leaned toward Doris. "Maybe something that could incriminate Henry?"

Doris pressed her lips together. "Unfortunately, I didn't see or hear anything. Bartholomew was sick, and I spent most of the night in the back room with him."

Everyone turned to look at the cat who simply stared back with his eerily intelligent green eyes.

"Is there anything else you can tell us about Rosa's murder?" Nans asked.

Doris shook her head, regret evident in her demeanor. "I wish I could. But the police have the killer in custody, so I imagine there's not much else that they need. I do hope he won't get off on some technicality."

"Oh, I'm sure the killer will be prosecuted to the fullest extent of the law. Well, I guess we've taken up enough of your time." Nans stood and they all followed her lead, pushing cats from their laps and replacing stuffed animals to their places.

Doris walked them to the door, and Nans turned back to her once they were all out in the hall and handed her a business card. "Give us a call if you think of anything that could be of help."

CHAPTER 15

"She was weird," Ida said, casting a glance back at the apartment house as she buckled herself into the back seat of Lexy's VW Beetle.

"That's what happens when an old lady lives alone," Ruth said. "Good thing we all have each other."

Ida smiled and patted Ruth's hand. "It is a good thing. What do you guys make of that business with the snake tattoo?"

Achoo!

"Helen, are you allergic to cats?" Nans asked.

"Apparently." Helen snapped her navy-blue patent leather purse open, pulled out a wad of tissues, and blew her nose. "Anyway, I think that's a good clue."

"Agreed," Nans said. "The question is, how do we find out who she is?"

"We know he was arrested for loitering around the bridge… maybe we could start there." Lexy had her blinker on to turn into the retirement center parking lot. Traffic was clear, but she didn't turn, thinking the ladies might want to go to the bridge to see if they could question someone now.

"Now?" Ida patted her stomach. "I'm getting a little hungry. Not sure I have the energy to interrogate homeless people."

Nans sighed. "I suppose we should regroup and think out our plan. I still have pastries from our clue session yesterday. Let's go to my place and get these new clues down."

"Sounds like a plan." Ida tapped Lexy on the shoulder. "Step on it. I'm hungry."

Lexy didn't have a lot of extra time to spend on the case. It was late afternoon, and she still had work at the bakery. She'd promised Jack she'd be on time for supper, but she supposed she could pop up to Nans for a few minutes. She hated not to be there when they went over clues.

She parked in the front lot, thankful to see that Helen's signs were still in the right places as they approached the entrance.

"Looks like Mario didn't mess with your signs," Ruth said as they walked through the lobby. "Maybe he's not as bad as you think, Helen."

"We'll see." Helen glanced around the lobby, frowning upon noticing it was empty of people she could press for a vote. "I just wish there was one more debate before people voted."

"Well, there's really not much more to debate about," Ida said, impatiently punching the button for the elevator. They usually took the stairs, but apparently, Ida couldn't wait that long for a snack.

"I did put out some coffee urns with a sign that said 'Free Coffee every Saturday if you Vote for Helen'. That ought to remind them who the best woman for the job is."

They filed into the elevator and got off on Nans's floor. Ida rushed inside once Nans opened the door and was rummaging in the fridge within seconds.

Ruth made coffee, Helen set out some pink crystal dessert plates with a pretty floral etched design, Ida filled a small gold-edged oval platter with the pastries, and they all sat at the dining room table.

Ida raised a brow and spoke with her mouth full. "You know, Helen, it would be even better if you put out some scones or muffins with the coffee urn."

Ruth practically choked on her muffin. "Are you

kidding? The first person there would take most of them."

Helen pursed her lips. "You know, that might not be a bad idea. I could—"

Nans interrupted them by loudly tapping the marker on the whiteboard. "Ladies! Let's focus on the investigation."

The ladies zipped their lips and focused their attention on the board, where the current clues and suspects were listed.

Nans had laid them out in columns, one for suspects and one for clues. Next to each item was an arrow pointing to pertinent information about that suspect or clue.

Ruth settled back in her chair, her keen eyes surveying the whiteboard over the rim of her gold-rimmed teacup. "It's really too bad Doris didn't see anything the night Rosa was killed."

"It is, but she did give us the snake tattoo clue." Nans wrote "snake tattoo" under the clues section and made an action item to follow it up then drew an arrow to the suspect column. Whoever had the snake tattoo might also be a suspect. "Do you all think the best way to start is by asking the homeless people under the bridge?"

"That might be kind of dangerous," Lexy said.

Jack would probably take a dim view of her interrogating the homeless people—some of them were just nice people who had fallen on hard times, but there were also some not-so-nice people who were into drugs.

"Maybe. Let's see what else shakes out." Nans stood back from the whiteboard to study the clues.

"I hate to say it, but it's starting to look like Henry really could be the killer," Ruth said.

Lexy nodded. "Jack seemed to think so too."

Ruth put down her teacup and leaned forward. "I think the heist and the murder could be related, but I'm not quite sure how or why. I'm certain the Circo Acrobata was involved."

Helen snorted. "I told you that Mario and his gang were no good."

Ruth glared at Helen. "It might not be Mario. There are plenty of acrobats in the show."

"But he was following us and peeking in my windows. Plus, he moved the signs, so that indicates that he's not above shady shenanigans," Helen said.

"She does have a point, Ruth." Ida cut the top off a cupcake and bit into it.

"Vinny said that the heist had a strategic mastermind behind it. Henry is good at chess, and that takes a lot of strategy. I think it would be smart of us to try to rule him out before we go around accusing someone else," Ruth said.

"Good point." Nans circled Henry's name in red then wrote "alibi" with a question mark beside it. "Henry's alibi seems to be very shaky. I think we should dig in to that."

"And don't forget the scandal!" Ida said.

"Yeah, he has a few counts against him," Ruth said. "And Doris seemed to think he was the killer. I know she didn't see anything, but over the years of living across the hall, she must have gotten a sense about Henry."

"I agree. He has a good motive with the life insurance payout, too, so this may not be related to the heist." Nans clicked the cap onto the marker. "We have to find out more about the alibi and the scandal in order to rule Henry out."

"Or prove him guilty," Lexy said. "But how do we check that out? Henry clammed up about the scandal, and he swears he was driving around."

Nans sat down at the table and grabbed a chocolate chip cookie from the platter. "Helen, don't you have a niece that works at the hospital?"

Helen nodded. "Two of them, actually. I'll text them and see if any of them know Henry or can get us some information."

"Perfect." Nans dunked the cookie into her tea.

"We still have to check out that other bakery," Ida said.

"Yes, maybe we should bring a picture of Henry and see if they recognize him. If he bought corn muffins, then I'm afraid that would be the final mark against him." Nans patted her lips with a napkin. "Is there anything else?"

Everyone shook their heads.

Nans glanced at the grandfather clock in the corner. "Okay then, let's break for the night. Lexy, will you come pick us up tomorrow?"

"Sure." Lexy supposed she could impose on Cassie to watch the bakery for one more day.

Helen pushed up from the table, gathering her plate and teacup and heading toward the kitchen. "I gotta run. I'm late for the cake-decorating class."

"I didn't know you had an interest in decorating cakes." Lexy wondered why Helen had never mentioned it, seeing as she owned a bakery and all. She and Cassie would have been happy to teach her.

"I don't, but those ladies in that class each have one vote. And the more I can get them to like me, the better my chances. See you all tomorrow!"

CHAPTER 16

The next morning, Lexy left Cassie with bakery duty and picked Nans and the ladies up. They were waiting in front of the retirement center, so she pulled to the curb and they folded themselves into her car. Helen gave one last glance at the campaign signs as Lexy pulled away.

"My niece Joanna is working in the ER. She said to come on down and she'll meet us there. She knows Henry." Helen twisted her neck to look out the window at her campaign signs as Lexy pulled out of the parking lot.

"And we can visit that bakery today too. Sugar Daddies. It's right on the corner of Granville and Elm, which is only a few blocks from the hospital," Ida said.

"Just those two stops though. We need a light investigating day today because tomorrow we vote for the community center president, and I want to have some time this afternoon for more campaigning." Helen brushed a piece of lint off her lapel. She'd worn a navy-blue suit, which Lexy had thought was odd, but now she realized she was probably trying to appear professional as part of her campaign strategy.

Nans caught Helen's eye in the rearview mirror. "I'm sure you'll have plenty of time to shake hands and kiss babies, but catching a killer is a bit more important."

Lexy drove the short distance to the local hospital and parked in the emergency room area. Since it was morning time, the waiting room was practically empty, consisting of a mother and small child and an elderly man who was sneezing into a hankie. The smell of rubbing alcohol pervaded the area.

Helen marched up to the desk. "Is Joanna Hammond in? Tell her Auntie Helen is here. She's expecting me."

The receptionist, who looked to be even older than Helen and Nans, narrowed her gaze. "What do you think this is, a real estate office? I don't summon employees, I check people in. Now step aside, as there are sick people that need my attention."

Helen glanced behind her. "There's no one in line behind me."

"So?" The woman pursed her wrinkled lips and patted her blue-tinted hair. "Someone could come in, and I don't want to be wasting time talking to you."

The door to the inner sanctum of the emergency room opened, and a pretty blonde in her mid-thirties wearing purple scrubs stepped out. "Auntie Helen?"

"Joanna!" Helen and Joanna hugged, and then Helen made the introductions.

The receptionist scowled at them. "Do you people mind? You're blocking access. Please go somewhere else."

Joanna pulled them aside and lowered her voice. "Don't mind Iris. Her bark is worse than her bite."

"Huh, if you say so." Ida glanced over her shoulder at the receptionist who was smirking at them as if she'd won some sort of battle.

"Your text said you wanted to ask me something, Auntie?" Joanna looked at them curiously.

"Yes, it's about a case." Helen sounded important. "One of the doctors here."

"Henry Maguire?" Joanna asked. "I know he was arrested. It's a shame because he was a good doctor. I can't imagine he killed his wife."

"We're not sure he did kill her," Ruth said.

"Really?" Joanna looked thoughtful. "Why do you say that? I thought he was arrested."

"He was, but his grandmother thinks he was set up," Ida said.

"We're looking into it for her." Nans glanced at the other emergency room occupants, and then pulled the group farther away from them. "Henry said he'd lost a patient that night and had to drive around to clear his head. No one can corroborate that since he was alone. So we were trying to get more information. Were you working that night? Did he seem upset?"

Joanna made a face. "What night was that?"

"The twenty-second," Nans said.

"The twenty-second. Hmm… I work in the ER Tuesday and Thursday so I'm not sure…"

Helen whipped out her smartphone and pulled up the calendar. "It's a Tuesday. Two weeks ago."

Joanna narrowed her eyes. "Are you sure? We haven't lost an ER patient in a few months."

Nans and the ladies exchanged a glance. "Are you sure? Maybe on another night that you didn't work."

Joanna shook her head. "No. Losing a patient is a big deal. There's counseling and reviews of what happened. I would know."

"So Henry lied?" Lexy asked.

"Sounds that way." Ida opened her purse and looked inside. "I'm fresh out of snacks. Looks like we're done here, so I guess we should head to the bakery."

Nans grabbed Ida's arm as she started to walk off. "We're not quite done yet." She turned to Joanna. "Did you know Henry well?"

"Not really. I worked with him a bit, but we weren't friends. He seemed like an okay guy, but that's what they said about Ted Bundy."

Ruth nodded. "Yeah, true. What about the scandal that Henry was involved in?"

Joanna's eyes clouded, and she glanced at the receptionist. "Where did you hear about a scandal?"

"From his grandmother, Muriel Maguire."

Joanna nodded. "Well, it wasn't really a scandal. More like a misunderstanding."

"What happened?" Nans asked.

Joanna glanced around again. "Look, I don't like to talk about hospital business like this, but some drugs were unaccounted for. But it was nothing. They took another look at the supply lists and it turned out they actually were accounted for."

Nans's radar pinged. "Really? Drugs?" She glanced around at the group. "Do you suppose this all has something to do with drugs?"

"Of course not," Joanna said. "The drugs were all accounted for."

"I know, dear. I was just thinking… Well, we won't keep you." Nans smiled at her. "Thank you for taking the time to talk to us."

"You're welcome." Joanna looked a bit uncertain, like she wished she hadn't mentioned the drugs. She hugged Helen and disappeared back through the door.

"Well that was interesting, now wasn't it?" Nans asked.

"Sure was. And you know what? I worked up an appetite talking to her. Let's get to that bakery and see if they have the offending corn muffins." Ida strutted toward the door without even waiting to see if they'd follow.

As they followed behind her, Nans said, "Looks like Henry might have had more going on than we thought."

CHAPTER 17

"Do you really think Henry is the killer?" Ruth asked as she pushed open the door to Sugar Daddies and gestured for the others to enter.

Inside the shop, the sweet smell of baking spiced the air. It was a small place with a black-and-white tile floor and gleaming pastry cases. It was clean, but there were no cafe tables to sit at and enjoy your purchase. Lexy felt selfishly happy about that—not that she was in competition with Sugar Daddies as it was a few towns over, but she liked to think the Cup and Cake was on par or better than the others in the area.

"I'm not convinced on that," Nans said. "The clues do seem to be pointing to him. And he has lied a few times. I just can't help but feel that if we can find out who bought the muffins, that will either clear him or seal his fate."

"Henry said the killer brought the muffins. That might have been a clever tactic because at first glance, it makes it sound like the killer was a visitor who brought muffins… but if Henry *is* the killer and he brought the muffins, it's not actually a lie," Helen said.

"But Henry is already in jail, so isn't it kind of anti-climactic to prove he's the killer?" Ida asked.

"Maybe, but at least we'll have tied the case up better than the police," Helen said.

"And we need proof to give to Muriel." Nans's eyes softened with sympathy for Muriel, and Lexy could imagine that if she were ever accused of anything, Nans would defend her to the end. That's what Muriel was doing for her grandchild. "It will be hard for her, but if Henry is the killer, she needs to have concrete evidence in order to accept it."

"I guess I would need to see that if it were my grandson being accused," Ruth said.

"But what does all this have to do with the missing drugs and the heist?" Helen asked. "There's still a tie-in with the Blondinis."

Nans nodded. "That's likely, but I suppose only Henry—or the killer—can answer that."

"A lot hinges on figuring out who brought the muffins," Ruth said.

"But it's very unlikely that someone would remember that purchase unless the buyer was a regular that the bakery staff knew personally." Lexy had dozens of customers that she knew personally, but if someone had only come in a few times or just once, she wouldn't remember what they bought or what they looked like. Hopefully the corn muffin buyer came frequently enough so as to be recognizable.

"Even if the bakery staff does remember who bought the muffins, how do we prove that person is the killer?" Ruth asked as they stood in front of one of the cases.

She had a point. Just proving someone bought muffins that were at the scene of the crime wasn't necessarily concrete evidence. The police would laugh them out of the station if they ever tried to insist the purchase of the muffins proved someone was a killer. But Lexy had an idea as to how it could help. "The sales system at the Cup and Cake records the items purchased and the time and date. If the killer used a credit card, their name would be linked too. Maybe we could use that time and date to prove that Henry—or whoever the killer is—had time to drive from here to the apartment and kill Rosa."

Nans nodded. "If there are CCTV cameras along the route, we might be able to tie that in."

"Nice try, but this bakery doesn't have that kind of system." Ruth pointed to an old cash register, and Lexy's hopes plummeted. She used to have the same system, and it only recorded the financial transaction and the time, not the item that was purchased.

"Darn," Nans said.

"Look at how thick the chocolate is on those biscotti. Lexy, you need to get on the ball with that." Ida tapped on the bakery glass, behind which sat a tray with several rows of golden biscotti, one end thickly coated with shiny dark chocolate.

Lexy frowned. Ida was right, that biscotti did have more chocolate. She made a mental note to see if she could up her game in that department.

"Lexy's biscotti are very nice. Every bakery has things that they excel at, but this one doesn't have cupcake tops at all." Helen's words placated Lexy. Cupcake tops were a unique and popular item in her bakery with people that wanted more frosting and less cake.

"And the cookies here are smaller," Ruth whispered. Lexy knew the ladies were trying to make her feel better about Ida's observation on the chocolate coating of the biscotti.

"But where are the muffins?" Nans glanced around the shop just as someone dressed in a white baker's shirt and puffy baker's hat came out with a tray of freshly baked muffins.

Ida gasped.

Helen choked.

Ruth snorted.

"Eureka!" Nans yelled much to the surprise of the baker.

Sitting on the tray was a dozen golden yellow corn muffins, and the tops were loaded with sparkling crystals of sugar.

"You must really love muffins," the baker said to Nans. She was a pleasant-looking middle-aged woman with turquoise-rimmed glasses and curly gray hair sticking out from under her baker's hat in unruly curls.

"We do. Especially the corn muffins with sugar crystals on top. You don't see those every day." Nans stood on tiptoes to see the tops of the muffins, and the baker lowered the tray so she could get a better look.

The baker smiled proudly at her muffins. "It's an original idea. I started making them a few months ago."

"Are they popular?" Ruth asked.

The baker frowned. "Well… umm… they haven't quite caught on yet, but they will."

"But some people must buy them." Nans gestured to the tray. "Otherwise you wouldn't keep making them."

"Oh, some people do." The baker slid the glass doors on a case and started rearranging things to put the muffins in.

"I suppose you remember the customers that bought these, especially since they are so unusual," Ruth said.

The baker glanced up through the glass. "I try to remember all my customers, but I suppose I do know the repeat corn muffin buyers."

Nans waited for her to put the last muffin in the case then asked, "Is one of the buyers a man in his early thirties, with glasses and dark-brown hair and a thin mustache?"

The baker looked thoughtful. "Hmmm, let me see… there's Mrs. Masserelli, from down the street. She's about ninety if she's a day but still spry. Then there's a pleasant young man with a man bun. Does your guy wear a man bun?"

Nans shook her head.

The baker shrugged. "Well, then I don't recall a pencil-mustache man, and the rest are all women.

Men tend to shy away from the crystal-sugar-topped items."

Lexy nodded in agreement. She'd noticed the same thing in her bakery, and it was probably because men didn't have the same sweet tooth as women. In general, they tended to go for the less sugary items like hermits, but there was always an exception. She supposed that Henry would stand out as one of those exceptions and thus the baker would remember him. Did that mean that Henry wasn't the killer, or did more than one bakery sell these corn muffins?

Helen stepped up to the counter. "What about an older man with arthritis in his hands?"

The baker shook her head. "Nope, don't remember him."

"Darn." Helen stepped away and perused the bakery case, apparently disappointed that her description of Mario Blondini didn't strike a chord.

"So, what can I get you?" the baker asked.

"I'll have one of those corn muffins." Ida nodded at the muffins she'd just placed in the case. "Wanna see what all the fuss is about."

"I'll have an eclair," Ruth said.

"Me too," Nans added.

"Nothing for me." Helen patted her stomach. "Trying to watch my weight."

"At least you aren't cutting out carbs like before," Ruth said. "You were hard to live with."

Helen scowled at Ruth. "I was not!"

"Were too," Nans and Ida said in unison.

Helen smiled. "Well, maybe I was a little."

Lexy also declined to order for the same reason, and they left with their purchases.

Out on the street, Ida reached into her sky-blue bag. Lexy only had white bags at her bakery, but this one was pretty. Maybe she would get pink, with her simple Cup and Cake logo stamped on the top, similar to the simple bee logo stamped on the bag Ida was holding.

Ida pulled out the corn muffin and took a bite. "This thing's not bad. Too bad the baker didn't recognize any of our suspects."

"That is disappointing." Nans pulled her eclair out of her bag, holding it carefully so as not to smudge chocolate all over her fingers. "Maybe we should show her a picture of Henry to be certain."

"And Mario," Helen piped up.

"She said only the man-bun guy and women bought the muffins, Helen." Ruth gave Helen a sideways glance. "You might have to admit that Mario is innocent."

"Henry or Mario could have had a woman buy

them for him," Ida suggested as she crunched on a sugar crystal.

"You mean, so that the police couldn't trace it and he could use the muffin to throw them off track?" Ruth considered this as she chewed on her eclair. "That would be something a strategist like Henry would do."

"Indeed," Nans agreed. "But either way, we need more proof. Henry would have known how to puncture Rosa's carotid artery with a butter knife, he really has no alibi, and he's a good strategist. He has at least one motive—the life insurance money—but might even have another if her death had something to do with the heist. Of course, we can't prove he bought the muffins, so that's disappointing."

"What if Henry really is the mastermind behind the heist and Rosa wasn't involved? Maybe she found out and threatened to tell," Ida said.

"That would be an additional motive," Nans agreed.

"Or maybe Rosa was involved and Henry wasn't and when he found out, he killed her in anger," Ruth said.

"Not as strong of a motive." Nans finished the last of her eclair and wiped the chocolate off her fingertips with a napkin.

Ruth sighed. "Right. Well, I suppose we are back to square one. Two steps forward and one step back."

"Not necessarily." Helen had stopped in front of a grimy storefront about fifty feet back, and they all turned at the sound of her voice.

"Why do you say that?" Nans asked.

"And what are you looking in there for? Are you thinking about getting a tattoo?" Ruth asked.

"'Helen for President' would look great on your bicep," Ida joked.

Helen turned and gave Ida a sour look. "If you must know, I think I might be on to something here." She pointed to the window. "Look."

They gathered around Helen, and Lexy squinted at the section Helen was pointing to, where a large piece of paper had samples of the tattoo artist's work. Smack-dab in the middle was a sample of a very detailed snake tattoo in vibrant greens, reds, and blacks, winding around an arm.

Nans turned toward the group. "Well ladies, looks like Helen just found our next clue."

CHAPTER 18

Lexy was surprised at the level of detail in the tattoos pictured on the walls of the shop. The artist was very talented, and each one was a mini work of art. She couldn't help but smile when picturing Jack's reaction if she showed up at home with a tattoo. Where would she put it? She'd probably get a cupcake, or maybe her logo.

"Do you have any samples of cat tattoos?" Lexy's thoughts were interrupted by Ida's question. She was at the reception desk talking to a young girl with silver-and-blue hair. The girl's pierced brows were raised almost to her hairline as she studied Ida, probably trying to determine whether or not she was serious.

"Dudly does a great tiger." The girl gestured

toward a painfully thin guy who was currently working on a parrot tattoo on the calf of a three-hundred-pound bald man. He glanced up and gave them a gold-capped-tooth smile.

"Hmmm, not a tiger. I was thinking more like a Persian or a Maine Coon." Ida flipped through a binder full of tattoo samples.

"Are all you ladies getting tattoos?" the girl asked. "We have a group rate…"

"We're not sure what we want," Nans said.

Lexy bit her tongue to keep from laughing at the image of the four ladies all with matching tattoos. Maybe they would get a magnifying glass with a thumbprint to match the logo on their business card. Where would they put it? Upper arm? Behind the neck? Of course, Ida would probably want it on her backside.

"We have some nice butterflies in this book." The girl flipped open another binder.

"I was thinking something more reptilian. We have an acquaintance with a snake tattoo like the one in the window. Now, what was her name…" Nans scrunched up her face as if trying to recall the person's name. "Rita?"

"No, I think it was Susan," Ida said, playing along with Nans's trick of trying to get the name of someone who'd had that tattoo done. This wasn't the first time Nans had conveniently pretended to forget the name of someone in order to get the person they were questioning to supply her with the actual name.

"Or was it Debbie?" Nans looked at the girl apologetically. "Sorry, the memory isn't what it used to be."

"Do you mean Ruby? Lives down on Elm Street in that old mill they made into apartments? I did the snake tattoo in the window on her," the girl said proudly.

Nans snapped her fingers. "Yes! That's it! Such a lovely tattoo. We were all admiring it."

The girl glanced at their wrinkled arms, probably trying to figure out just how she'd replicate such an intricate work of art on the flabby skin. "I guess I could do a group deal on that. It takes a long time. Would be quite a few visits."

"Oh dear." Helen sighed, looking at her watch. "We don't have a long time. I need to get back on the campaign trail. I'm running for senior community center president, you know."

"Yeah." Ida chewed her bottom lip. "Maybe we should think more on this."

"Good idea. Sorry dear, you know how us old ladies are. Change our minds a lot." Nans headed for the door with Ruth, Ida, and Helen on her heels. Lexy smiled apologetically at the girl behind the counter and followed them out.

"Thanks for driving us over here, Lexy. I know you have a business to run," Ida said as they pulled up in front of the brick building on Elm Street.

"No problem. It's a slow time of year, and Cassie can handle things without me." It was the truth, but Lexy had another reason to want to accompany them —she wanted to be there just in case the ladies got into trouble. Ruby was a suspect, and you never knew when things could turn sour. Even though they were very spry and able to handle themselves, they were getting a bit older. And she had to admit, she also wanted to be in the thick of things with the case.

"This looks like a nice building," Helen said as they stood at the glass entrance, scanning the list of names on the brass plate that had the buzzers. The mill was a hundred years old, and though it was recently renovated into apartments, they'd kept a lot of the old charming details, like the aged brick and wide pine floors.

"This must be her. Ruby Dewalt." Ida pointed to a

name card. The tattoo girl hadn't given them a last name, but how many Ruby's could there be?

Helen pressed the buzzer, and they waited.

"Huh, maybe she's not home. Now what?" Ruth asked.

"I guess we could come back later." Helen started to turn away just as an elderly man in a tweed jacket and cane came out. He tipped his hat at them and continued on. Ida put the toe of her shoe in the door and waited until he disappeared around the corner.

"Or we could go in and check the place out." Ida slipped inside. Nans turned to the rest of them, who shrugged and followed her in.

The hallways had the scent of old wood and lemon pledge. The walls were painted a trendy slate gray. The ceilings were ten feet tall and had exposed duct work.

"At least the landlord keeps things updated," Ruth said. "These are newer colors, according to the decorating magazines."

"The buzzer said she was in 204. That must be on the second floor." Ruth headed toward a stairway, and they walked up one flight then found the door.

"Looks like all the other doors." Ida glanced around the hallway. "No new clues here."

"Let's just knock… maybe she didn't hear us

before because she was in the shower. That happened to me once when maintenance came to fix my leaky kitchen faucet. Imagine my surprise to find Herbert in my kitchen when I walked in there wearing only a towel."

"Imagine Herbert's surprise…" Ida said.

Nans knocked. "Ruby? Hello?"

She knocked harder, and the door creaked open.

"Uh oh…" Helen said. "This doesn't bode well. Who leaves their door open?"

"Who gets a snake tattoo all over their arm?" Ida answered.

"Good point." Nans pushed the door further open, and they stepped in.

As soon as they stepped in, Lexy knew something bad had happened. A lamp lay on the floor, casting an eerie light on the wall. The kitchen counter stools were knocked over. A black leather purse lay on the floor next to a chair, its contents spilling out of the top. And a foot stuck out from behind the breakfast bar.

They rushed over to find a dark-haired woman in a pool of blood. Her clouded eyes stared at the ceiling. Nans squatted to feel for a pulse, but everyone knew the girl was long gone.

"Well, looks like that lead is gone." Ida pointed to

the snake tattoo on the woman's arm. "Now we'll never be able to ask her what her association with Henry was."

"If she even had one with him," Ruth said.

"Look at her neck and the weapon." Nans pointed to a blood-covered steak knife that lay beside the victim. "She was stabbed similar to Rosa."

"It would be easier to puncture the artery with a steak knife than a butter knife, but that does seem to indicate the same killer," Helen said.

"If so, it clearly wasn't Henry." Nans stood up, careful not to step in the blood. "Blood is dry—she's been here a while."

"We need to figure out if the two murders are related." Ida wandered over to the kitchen counter and started shuffling through the mail.

"Ida! What are you doing? We need to call the police." Helen had her phone in her hand and was already thumbing in 911.

"Of course we should." Ida held an envelope up to the light as if to see the contents while Helen completed the call. She put it down and continued her perusal. "But we can't leave until they come and question us, so we might as well look around while we are waiting."

Lexy glanced down at the body, an uncomfortable

feeling washing over her. "It doesn't feel right to poke through her things when she's laying right here."

"We're not going to poke. We're just going to look." Nans glanced at Ida. "And we should be careful not to touch anything. Fingerprints and all."

"Right." Ida dropped the letter she was holding.

"We may have to solve this murder, too, and we'll need to get all the clues we can," Nans said as she surveyed the room with the eye of an expert private detective. "This is a unique opportunity to be first on the scene."

Good point. Lexy walked around the room looking for anything out of place. Maybe she'd get lucky and find a cuff link on the floor or a cigarette butt in the ashtray that could lead to the identity of the killer.

"Well, looky here!" Helen gestured to a collage of framed photos that were displayed on a side table. "Looks like maybe Doris Pettigrew was wrong about who Ruby was coming to visit."

Lexy joined her. The photos showed a smiling Ruby with a group of people, one of whom was Rosa Maguire. They were standing arm in arm, clearly very friendly.

"That's Rosa, and they look pretty chummy," Ida stated the obvious.

"Doesn't look like Ruby would want to kill Rosa. At least not in that picture." Ruth pointed to another picture in the back. "Check out this one."

The picture, in a fancy etched silver frame, showed Ruby, Rosa, and four others dressed in sparkly bodysuits and standing next to a large trampoline. "Looks like they performed in the Circo Acrobato together."

"Ruby must have been one of the 'family' that Henry talked about," Helen said.

"He said that Rosa was worried about the family. Maybe there was an argument between her and Ruby and it turned deadly." Ida looked hopeful.

"Ruby could have killed Rosa, but then who killed Ruby?" Nans asked.

Ida's hopeful look turned to disappointment. "Good point. But this does prove that they must have been close friends."

"I'll say." Ida was crouched near the overturned purse, leafing through the pages of a small book with the eraser end of a pencil. "Looks like Ruby was an old-fashioned girl despite her love of skin art. This here is a calendar. No electronic phone calendars for her. She penciled her appointments in."

"Nothing wrong with that," Ruth huffed. "I still

use a paper calendar. I love those little ones you get at the pharmacy. Mine has pink roses on it."

Ida flipped back to the cover. "This one has butterflies. I was expecting snakes, but maybe they don't make them with snakes. Anyway, it's not what's on the cover that's interesting. It's what she has written in here. Dinner with Rosa."

Nans's head whipped around to look at Ida. "Rosa? Could it be Rosa Maguire?"

Ida shrugged. "There's no last name, but they look pretty chummy in the picture, so I think that's a safe assumption."

Helen peered at the book over Ida's shoulder. "That date is a few days before Rosa's murder. Could they have been meeting about something related?"

"If they were, it wouldn't be a stretch to conclude that whoever killed Rosa also killed Ruby." Nans pressed her lips together and tilted her head, deep in thought. "What if Rosa and Ruby knew something, and someone didn't want them to tell?"

"If that's the case, then Henry isn't the killer." Ruth gestured toward the body in the kitchen. "He couldn't have killed Ruby because he's in jail."

"Which means we better start paying more attention to our other suspects," Nans said.

"I knew it!" Helen said. "This is related to the

Circo Acrobata and possibly to that heist that Vinny told us about. And who else was in the Circo? Mario! We already know that he's a shady character, and now, he seems to be right in the thick of things."

"Now, don't be so quick to throw him under the bus," Ruth said. "There are plenty of people in the Circo Acrobata family. And for all we know, Henry is behind it all, the strategic mastermind pulling strings from his jail cell."

Helen put her hands on her hips. "That may well be, but if that's the case, then someone else is surely involved. Unless Ruby's death is not related to Rosa's."

"We do have to consider that they aren't related," Nans said.

"Yeah, well, let's save our considering for when we are back at your place." Ida had gone over to the window and was looking out. "The cops are here."

Everyone made a beeline for the door, which Nans opened so they could all step out into the hall. "Okay everyone, put on your innocent old lady faces and pretend like we've been out in the hallway all this time so they don't think we were snooping around inside."

～

Jack was the first to come around the corner. His footsteps faltered, and he let out an exaggerated sigh. "Not you people."

"We can't help it if we're always in the wrong place," Ida said.

"Were you snooping around inside?" Jack glanced at Lexy who gave him a wan smile.

"No. Well, I mean, maybe we looked at a few things before we realized there was a dead body," Nans said.

"And just exactly why are you here?" Jack gestured for the rest of his crew to get to work inside. He leaned against the wall, arms crossed over his chest as he waited for their answer.

Nans lowered her voice. "We were following a lead in the Maguire case."

"So Ruby Dewalt is a person of interest in that case?" Jack asked.

Nans nodded. "I guess her place here is in your jurisdiction then?"

"Yep. I'm going inside to check it out. You guys stay put. I still want to talk to you." Jack entered the apartment, and the ladies crowded in behind him just like they weren't supposed to. He turned and looked at them, opened his mouth, probably to tell them to wait outside, then shook his head as he thought better of it. He knew them well enough to know his warning might not stick. "Don't get in anyone's way, and don't touch anything."

As Jack and the police processed the body, Nans whispered, "This is good. If Jack will be investigating this murder, we might be able to help him."

"At least maybe he will share some clues," Ida said.

"And Jack is a good cop. He could solve this murder where the other cops have the wrong guy," Ruth whispered.

Lexy beamed with pride. She knew Jack was a good cop, but it was always nice to hear it from others. "We should fill him in."

"Oh, we will," Nans said absently, her ear cocked toward the kitchen as she probably tried to listen in. Lexy wouldn't be surprised if she tweaked her hearing aids up a notch so as to be able to hear any hushed conversations.

"Okay, so, tell me again how you came to be in this apartment with the deceased," Jack said.

"As I said, we were following a lead." Nans filled Jack in on how the nosey neighbor had seen someone with a snake tattoo visiting Henry and how they'd found the tattoo parlor while looking for corn muffins.

Jack's eyes narrowed. "So, let me get this straight. You were looking for a special type of corn muffin because you think the killer brought them, and beside the muffin shop was a tattoo parlor that had a snake tattoo that was seen on someone visiting Henry."

"That's right." Nans nodded.

"So the deceased, Ruby, would have known about the bakery. Maybe she brought the corn muffins to Rosa," Jack said.

"She could have. They knew each other." Ruth pointed to the pictures on the table.

Jack looked them over then glanced back. "So maybe she saw something the night Rosa was killed and that's why she was killed."

"Maybe, or she could have been up to something with Rosa and that's why they both got killed," Ruth said.

Jack nodded. "And what else did you guys just happen to see here while you weren't snooping around?"

"We might have noticed that she had an appointment with Rosa shortly before Rosa died." Ida pointed to the contents of the purse, and Jack let out another sigh. Before he could lecture them about contaminating crime scenes, a uniformed policeman came up beside him.

"We're almost done with the body. Looks like she's been dead sixteen hours, give or take fifteen minutes on either side. Billy is done with photos, and he's going to start in here." The man looked at Lexy and the ladies.

"Sounds good. These ladies were just leaving." Jack turned to them. "You can go home. Don't worry, I know where to find you, and if you do anything that might impede the investigation, you will not like the consequences." He winked at Lexy. "Especially you."

Lexy's stomach did a little flip. At least he wasn't mad. And by the look in his eye, the consequences might not be so dire either. Naturally, she would never do anything to mess up the investigation for him, but it was good to know she wasn't in trouble. She made a mental note to make sure that whatever Nans and the ladies did would only help and not harm what the police were doing.

A slight pang of guilt bubbled up about her trip to the prison, but technically, she didn't go to visit a prisoner, so technically, she didn't break her promise. Still, maybe she should come clean on that. Not now, though. Later, when the timing was better.

"Did you hear that?" Helen whispered as they filed out into the hallway. "That policeman said that

Ruby was killed sixteen hours ago. Mario could be the killer."

"What makes you say that?" Ruth asked.

Helen looked at her watch. "I've been checking the time pretty regularly because tonight is the voting for community center president, and I have to visit some of the less mobile residents and see if I can help them get to the center to vote."

"And this makes Mario suspicious because…" Ruth gave Helen the side-eye.

"Sixteen hours ago was ten o'clock yesterday. That was when we were peering into Mario's windows. Didn't you notice the house was empty?" Helen asked.

"Well, it did seem empty, but just because Mario wasn't home doesn't mean he was here killing Ruby," Ruth pointed out. "And besides, the dining room was set up for a buffet. Who sets out the food then goes off and kills someone?"

"Maybe someone who is trying to create a false alibi," Helen said. "Now, if you don't mind, Lexy, you'll need to step on it. I want to get back and secure some last-minute votes!"

ack at the retirement center, Helen didn't waste any time on her goal of getting more votes. She spied potential victims watching TV as soon as they entered the lobby and headed over.

"Celia! Ellen! Mary! So good to see you!" Helen exuberantly shook hands with the blue-haired ladies, who seemed a bit perturbed at being interrupted during their soap opera. It was General Hospital, and Lexy couldn't blame them—Luke was up to something on his casino boat, and she was sure it was no good.

"Have you had a chance to think of who you want for community center president?" Helen stood in front of them, blocking the view of the television.

"Not really." Celia tried to peer around Helen.

"Don't forget that I promise to have free coffee on Saturdays." Helen leaned in and lowered her voice. "I can really come through with my promises, unlike some people who might promise the moon and not be able to deliver."

"Helen, are you coming?" Nans punched the button for the elevator.

Helen glanced over. "In a minute." She looked back down at the women, who were craning to watch TV around her. "Now the coffee isn't the only thing I will do, of course—"

"If we promise to vote for you, will you let us watch our show?" Ellen asked.

Helen glanced behind her at the TV. "Your show? Oh, umm… sure. A vote is a vote no matter how I get it, I suppose."

"Great, then we all promise to vote for you." Mary waved her hand for Helen to step to the side.

Helen shrugged. "Great then! See you there. Tonight at seven p.m.!" She hurried off toward the elevator. Everyone was already inside, and Ida impatiently held the door for her.

"About time," Ida said as she repeatedly punched the button to close the door.

Nans could barely wait for the doors to open on the second floor before she bolted to her apartment, shoved the key in the lock, and pushed the door open. She was at the whiteboard before the rest of them even got inside.

"The exciting event of another victim really sheds a different light on this case." Nans made another column and added the information about Ruby.

"It seems to indicate that Henry really is innocent just like Muriel thought," Ruth said.

"Do we have any snacks?" Ida yelled from the kitchen. "I can't think about clues on an empty stomach."

"In the bottom drawer," Nans yelled back. "Now, let's go over what we know."

"We know that both victims knew each other and were in the Circo Acrobata." Helen glanced at her watch.

"Don't worry, Helen, we still have a few hours left before voting," Ruth said. "And we know that Henry couldn't have killed Ruby."

"And we know that Vinny thinks that the Circo Acrobata people had something to do with the Broadmoore Heist," Lexy said.

Nans nodded. "Putting two and two together, we can assume the deaths had something to do with the heist. Either the two women were involved or they knew something."

Ida came out of the kitchen with a serving tray full of cut-up vegetables and some dip, her disgusted expression indicating her disappointment in the snacks. The smell of percolating coffee wafted out from behind her, and Lexy heard the old-fashioned coffee urn gurgle. "I could only find these vegetables. Guess we ate all the pastries."

"Veggies are good for you!" Helen picked up a carrot and chomped off a bite as if to prove her point. "I think we've had enough pastry with all the bakeries we've been visiting."

"I haven't." Ida picked up a celery stick and made a face before nibbling on the end.

"Ladies!" Nans tapped the marker on the whiteboard. "Can we stick to the case? We've had two murders, and I'd like to solve it before there's a third."

"Fine," Ida said. "Let's assume the heist and the murders are related. All we need to do is figure out if one of our suspects has the loot from the heist, and we have our man."

"Maybe." Nans thought this over. "But what if Ruby or Rosa had the loot, and the killer did away with them to take it?"

"Maybe Rosa and Henry had it and Ruby killed

Rosa and took it, and then someone found out Ruby had it and killed her so *they* could take it," Helen said.

"Either way, if we find the loot, we find the killer," Ida said.

"Right. And what was stolen in the heist? Valuable antiques. Vases. Paintings." Helen nodded at them knowingly. "And whose windows were we looking in earlier that had antiques, vases, and paintings? Mario Blondini!"

"Lots of people have vases and antiques," Ruth pointed out.

"All the clues point to Mario. He's sneaky, he has antiques, he was in the Circo Acrobata—"

The sound of a bag crinkling interrupted Helen, and all eyes turned to Ida, who looked up at them sheepishly. "Sorry, I got hungry for real food. I only have part of a corn muffin left or I'd share." She shoved a muffin top into her mouth and crinkled the bag into a ball.

"Wait a minute." Lexy reached for the bag, her eyes on the blue bee logo. Now she remembered where she'd seen that before. On a box in Mario's dining room. She smoothed the wrinkles in the bag and held it up. "Helen might be onto something. I've been looking at the logos on the bags so I could compare them to the Cup and Cake logo, and I saw this logo on a pastry box in Mario's dining room."

"Which proves that Mario was at Sugar Daddies—the bakery that sells the corn muffins with sugar crystals on top!" Helen was more excited than the day she won the big prize at bingo.

Ida, not so much. She made a face and shook her head. "I don't know, Helen, that seems kind of flimsy."

"No, it's perfect! All we have to do is prove that Mario is the killer, then he will be disqualified from the election, and I'll win by default! We need to get a confession out of him right away!" Helen jumped up from the table and ran out the door before anyone could stop her.

CHAPTER 20

Lexy and the others rushed out of Nans's place after Helen. She was fast and had beat them to the elevator. The doors were just closing, so they ran down the stairs and tumbled out onto the sidewalk just in time to see Helen turning the corner that led to Mario's place.

"Helen, wait!" Nans yelled, but either Helen didn't hear, or she was so focused on getting a confession from Mario that she didn't want to slow down. They had no choice but to pick up the pace to try to catch her.

"Darn it! I don't think she's thought this through. If she had, she might have doubts about Mario being the killer. If she confronts him, she may be making a big mistake," Nans said, her orthopedic sneakers squeaking on the pavement as they rounded the corner at a jog.

"She seems convinced." Lexy wondered what Nans meant. Helen had made a good case for Mario being the killer, and Lexy had seen the bakery box with her own eyes.

"Yes, but remember, the killer must have means, motive, and opportunity… oh dear, she's knocking on the door!" Nans forged ahead with a burst of speed that surprised Lexy. They were about twenty feet away from the door when Mario Blondini opened it.

He blinked at Helen, his surprise turning to suspicion as his gaze drifted to the others who were racing to join them. "What is going on here? Does this have to do with the election?"

"I think you know what it has to do with." Helen pushed her way inside, and Mario stumbled back. He looked genuinely confused.

"I'm sorry, Helen, but I'm not up for visitors. We've had a death in the family," Mario said weakly as the rest of them piled into the foyer.

Now that Lexy was closer, she could see Mario's red-rimmed eyes and shaking hands. It appeared as if the poor man really was grieving, and Lexy had a pang of sympathy for him. Still, she couldn't help but look around the foyer to see if any of the things stolen in the heist were lying about.

It was a large round space with a honey-pine floor and paneled mahogany walls fit more for a mansion than a Brook Ridge Falls retirement villa. It was decorated quite tastefully with antique touches here and there. A tall cut-glass vase on a marble-topped table held a spray of colorful flowers in purple, yellow, and orange. Their sweet smell hung lightly in the air. A collage of gilt-framed paintings of hunting dogs adorned one wall, landscapes another. But all the items appeared as if they'd been there for a while and weren't just placed there to hide in plain sight after the heist.

Nans grabbed Helen's arm. "Now Helen, I think you should—"

Helen shook her off. "We know about the death. Are condolences in order or…" Helen let her voice drift off as she glanced around the foyer, probably scoping it out for heist loot like Lexy had just done.

"Or what?" Mario asked.

"Or maybe you're glad she's out of the way?"

Mario gasped. "How can you say such a thing? She was a lovely girl. Okay, maybe a bit on the wild side, but still."

"Helen, really—" Nans made a futile attempt to silence Helen but was interrupted again.

"What's with all these antiques here? Did you just get them?" Helen ignored Nans completely.

"What?" Mario looked confused at the change in topic. To tell the truth, Lexy was too. "Are you on something? Too much of that free coffee you are offering as a campaign promise, perhaps?"

"No. I'm not on anything. Except a quest for justice! Where'd you get all these antiques?" Helen gestured around the foyer and then walked over to stand in the doorway to the dining room. "And these in here."

Mario sighed. "Well, if you must know, they are family heirlooms. The blue china in the china cabinet was my grandmother's. And this credenza here belonged to my uncle." He pointed a gnarled finger at a marble-topped cabinet with carved deer that sat along one wall of the foyer. "Various vases and paintings are from other relatives. The family has traveled extensively with the Circo Acrobata, and we pick things up."

Helen crossed her arms over her chest and tapped her foot. "You didn't get them from the heist?"

"Heist? What heist? What in the world are you

talking about?" Mario glanced from Helen to the rest of them. "Are you people mad?"

"Helen, if you would just listen—" Nans tried again, but Helen put her hand out and shushed her.

"I'll listen when Mario explains where he was yesterday when Ruby was killed!" Helen said.

Mario looked offended but also tired. "Fine, if you must know, I was meeting with my lawyer at that time. I had some matters to tend to, then we were going to have a nice brunch back here. Endora was setting it all up."

"Aha!" Helen pointed at him. "This proves it! How would you know what time Ruby was killed if you weren't the killer? See, that was what's known as a trick question, and you fell right into my trap."

"Umm... the police told me, of course. It was just terrible news." Mario's eyes misted, and Lexy felt another pang of guilt.

That took the wind out of Helen's sails. "Well, surely you had motive." But now she didn't sound so certain of that.

"Helen, stop." Nans must have felt bad for Mario, too, because her tone was a little more forceful this time. "I think you might be barking up the wrong tree. The killer had to be able to kill Rosa easily with a butter knife."

"And Ruby with a steak knife. Though that looked a bit easier because it's sharper," Ida said.

"So what? Mario is in the Circo Acrobata. I'm sure he did a stint as a knife thrower. Surely he knows exactly where the carotid artery is because he'd want to avoid hitting it." Helen looked quite pleased with herself for coming up with this.

"Indeed," Nans said. "But it takes a steady hand and lots of strength to push a butter knife into the neck of a struggling victim. Look at Mario's hands. He has arthritis. It wouldn't be possible for him to be the killer."

Helen's gaze pivoted to Mario's gnarled fingers, and her face fell in disappointment. "I... but... he moved my signs and has been trying to undermine me!"

Mario held his hands up, his face sad. "Yes, sadly I've been afflicted with this. I had to quit the Circo Acrobata because I could no longer perform. I thought my life was over until this campaign for community center president. It's given me a new lease on life. I'm sorry if I've been a little overzealous in my campaigning, Helen."

Helen looked even more disappointed. "But..."

"Never mind all that," Ida said. "If Mario isn't the killer, then who is?"

Nans pressed her lips together. "Well, it would have to be someone that was good with knives. Someone who knew where the carotid artery is located. Someone strong enough to win a struggle with Rosa and Ruby."

"And someone who was involved in the heist," Ruth added.

"What heist?" Mario repeated. "Why do you people keep talking about a heist?"

But before anyone could answer him, William appeared in the doorway. His expression turned into a menacing scowl when he noticed them.

Lexy remembered the way William had threatened them with the knife and bragged about his skills. "Someone like William, perhaps?"

William hurried to Mario's side. "Who are you people? Are they bothering you, Uncle Mario? Do you want me to get rid of them?"

Lexy wasn't particularly fond of the way William said "get rid of them," and judging by the expression on Nans's face and the way Ida was sidling toward the door, neither were they.

"I think our visit is just about over." Mario raised a brow at the ladies.

"Wait a minute. Aren't you the busybodies I caught looking in our windows yesterday?" William turned to Mario. "Should I call the cops on them?"

"Ha! Nice try! We should call the cops on *you*!" Helen took a step forward, but when William reached into his pocket where he presumably kept his knife, she stopped. "You have means, motive, and opportunity! You have access to the house and could stash antiques here. It's cluttered, and no one would notice."

William did a good job of looking confused. "What are you talking about?"

Helen put her hands on her hips. "I think you know exactly what I'm talking about, young man."

"Uhh… Helen, maybe we shouldn't be too hasty," Nans said.

"Nonsense. He's young enough to win a struggle and doesn't have any ailments that would impede him," Helen said.

"But I don't think—" Lexy started, but Helen waved her off.

"I should have thought about it before. William is the knife thrower in the Circo Acrobata. He probably could have taken Rosa out from across the room. Poor kid never saw it coming." Helen wagged her finger in William's face. "You should be ashamed of yourself."

"What's with these ladies? I think they're unstable. Especially this one." William pointed to Helen. "Isn't she the one running against you for president of the community center? You said she was an admirable opponent, but I think she's nuts. I don't think she's a good candidate for president of anything."

Helen's eyes softened as she looked at Mario. "You said I was an admirable opponent?"

Mario shrugged. "You run a tough campaign."

"Oh, thanks." Helen's gaze shifted back to William. "Then I'm sorry about your family tragedies and especially sorry that we'll have to have your nephew arrested."

William sighed and crossed his arms over his chest. "See, told you. She's nuts."

"Oh no, I know exactly what—"

"Helen!" Nans barked. "Earlier you were so sure Mario was the killer because he wasn't at home when Ruby was killed."

"We know that because we were peeking in the windows," Ida interrupted. "We saw the big buffet set up, but no one was here. Speaking of which, you wouldn't happen to have any leftover pastries from that? Looked like a lot of food."

"Ida! Not now!" Helen turned to Nans. "Yes, exactly. We knew Ruby's time of death, and since I was very aware of the time so I could stay on schedule for my campaign, I know for a fact that Mario wasn't here at the house during that time."

"Yes, but then you also know who *was* here." Nans wiggled her finger in William's direction. "Remember, he caught us snooping."

Helen's brows knit together, and she hesitated for a beat. "Well, now that you mention it, I suppose you're right. So William has the best alibi. Us."

Ruth had sidled over, closer to Mario. Lexy guessed now that he wasn't the main suspect, he was fair game for flirtation. But her expression was clouded. "Well, if it wasn't Mario, and it wasn't William, then who else could it have been?"

"Well, well, well. If it isn't your pesky opponent and her little entourage. What brings you elderly ladies here?" Endora stood in the hallway that led off to the right. Somehow, she'd snuck up despite the fact that she was wearing two-inch silver stilettos to complement her clingy black jumpsuit. She did not look happy to see them.

"Apparently, they came to accuse Uncle Mario of killing Rosa," William said.

Endora scowled at them with eyes as bottomless as a raven's but not nearly as intelligent. "That's preposterous! What makes you even think that?"

"We think it's connected to the Broadmoore heist, for one," Ida said.

"And he knows where the carotid artery is, for two," Ruth added.

"But then we realized it can't be him," Nans said.

Endora raised a brow and slinked toward the foyer table. Something about her demeanor set Lexy on edge. Was she up to something?

"So what are you still doing here, then?" Edora stopped at the vase and took a deep sniff of the flowers. Lexy relaxed. Apparently Endora was only going over to sniff the flowers. Endora then turned to Mario. "Why haven't you kicked them out?"

Mario hesitated. "Well, that seems a bit impolite."

Endora leaned against the table and crossed her arms over her chest. "Seems to me nosey little old ladies shouldn't go around casting accusations. It could be dangerous."

Uh-oh, that sounded threatening. Lexy glanced at Nans, who had also picked up on the tone. Helen and Ruth seemed oblivious. Ida was glancing longingly into the dining room.

"We thought we had a good case." Helen glanced at her watch. "Oh dear, only two hours until the vote. I suppose I better hit the campaign trail."

"Not so fast." Endora stepped in front of her, blocking the way to the door. "I want to know exactly what you ladies are up to. I know you've been investigating Rosa's death, and now that you know Mario wasn't the killer, do you finally believe it's Henry?"

"Oh, no," Helen said. "It can't be Henry. The same person that killed Rosa killed Ruby."

Endora shook her head. "No. Ruby was killed by one of her lowlife friends."

"She's probably right," Nans said. "We should go."

Helen frowned. "What do you mean? Earlier you said it was the same killer. Someone who was involved in the heist, and that's why we thought it was Mario and then William, because the loot from the heist could easily be hidden here."

"I've told you, these are all family heirlooms." Mario glared around the room, his gaze falling on a painting. "Hmm... except I don't remember this one."

"You're getting forgetful," Nans said. "Happens to the best of us. Okay, gang, let's get going. Helen has hands to shake and babies to kiss."

"Wait a minute." Helen's gaze was fixed on the painting that Mario couldn't remember. "We need to think about our suspect pool. It should be very small with all the criteria. The heist. The Circo Acrobata. Has to be someone who would know just where to place that butter knife and strong enough to get it to tear through flesh..."

Lexy followed Nans's gaze. She was watching Endora like a hawk. Lexy saw again the scars on her face and remembered when she'd turned her head so as to protect her neck against getting cut from the sign. It was a built-in reflex she likely had from being the target in the knife-throwing act in the Circo Acrobata. Endora would know exactly how to protect those vulnerable arteries in her neck. Which meant, she also knew exactly where those arteries were. Not to mention that she was an acrobat and could have gotten around the security laser. She clearly still kept in shape. She also had strong hands and wasn't home when Ruby was killed. But it was just a theory. They needed more evidence before they could accuse her. If Helen continued her train of thought, though, they were all going to be in a bit of trouble.

"Yeah, someone who knew Rosa and Ruby well enough that those girls would let them right into their places and set the table for coffee and muffins," Ida said. "And someone strong enough to overtake them when going in quick for the kill. There are really only a couple of people who would fit that description."

Endora whipped the drawer in the console open and pulled out a gun, pointing it straight at them. "That's right. I did it. Are you busybodies happy now?"

"Endora!" Mario looked shocked. "What are you doing? Put that gun down."

"Isn't it obvious? Now that these old bats have figured things out, the cat is out of the bag." Endora's eyes turned even colder, and she looked at Mario with disdain. "You don't think I was hanging around you because I really liked you, did you?"

"Well… I…" Mario's face pinched. The uncaring words had clearly hurt him.

"Yeah, exactly." Endora's laugh was brittle. "You were a means to an end. I had to have somewhere to stash the loot."

Mario glanced at the painting he couldn't remember owning.

"You're the brains behind the heist!" Ida said.

Nans gave Lexy a look, indicating she'd come to that conclusion about five minutes ago when she tried to shut Helen up.

"Yeah, planned it for months. I've kept up with my acrobatic training." Endora gestured to her slim body. "One needs to be able to leap, to do backbends and cartwheels to sidestep the laser security beams. And don't even ask about the mini-trampoline. That's what got me inside."

"Mini-trampoline?" Ida asked. "You mean like a rebounder? You know those things are good for the lymph nodes. Great exercise. So, you got into the Broadmoore house somehow and then rebounded into an open area of the security and acrobated your way to the loot?"

Endora nodded, clearly pleased with herself. "Took a lot of choreography to plan that."

"You did all this alone?" William asked.

"Nah, I enlisted the aid of Georgie, Bella, and Julio." Endora tilted her head as if thinking. "Oh, and some guy that Julio knew. Vinny. He was our fall guy."

"Who are Georgie, Bella, and Julio?" Helen asked.

"More members of the family. Of course, we were going to have to wait a while to get all the money from the sale of the items. We were selling things off a little at a time so as not to raise suspicion. I had the perfect place to store the rest of them—right here in plain sight." Endora gestured toward the vases with the flowers and the painting Mario didn't remember.

"You mean you've been using me to store stolen goods?" Mario asked.

Endora smiled. "Yeah, sorry, sweetie. But you'd

find out sooner or later that you're not my type. I prefer someone much younger."

"Well, that's a bit of a relief," Mario said. "You're not really my type, either. Hard to keep up with, plus you're not really warm and fuzzy. And that explains why there were some vases and antique items here I did not remember. I thought I was going senile."

Ruth patted his arm. "Memory lapses happen to the best of us, Mario."

Mario smiled at Ruth, then his expression turned to a frown as his gaze drifted to Endora. "And you killed Rosa and Ruby."

"I had to. They were onto me. Rosa had discovered some of the items here and was asking a lot of questions. After Rosa died, Ruby got it in her head that Henry was innocent and started asking a lot of questions that made me uncomfortable." Endora shrugged. "I did what I had to do."

Mario shook his head. "But you said that you heard Henry and Rosa fighting and he threatened to kill her? You lied about that?"

Endora shrugged. "He was the perfect person to frame. I happen to know he has other scandalous secrets."

Lexy remembered Muriel mentioning something about a scandal and how Henry clammed up when they asked him about it. But if the scandal wasn't related to the heist or the murder, then what was his big secret? She didn't have time to dwell on that, though, because Endora looked like she was getting a bit anxious with the gun.

"You let an innocent man go to jail." Mario looked at Endora with disgust. "You're despicable."

"Well, a girl has to look out for number one," Endora said.

"And you killed two members of our family!" William added.

"*Your* family, not mine. Oh, sure, Ruby and Rosa were members of the *extended* Circo Acrobata family, but they were going to turn me in. What family member does that?" Endora asked. "And if Ruby had just minded her own business, she'd still be alive. When I got wind she was going to prove Henry was innocent, I had no choice but to kill her."

"How could you kill those innocent girls?" Mario asked.

"Actually, it was easy. I guess keeping in shape paid off because it wasn't hard to over-come them even though they were younger. Of course, it did help knowing exactly where to puncture the neck." Endora pointed to a spot on her own neck. "They bleed out pretty quick if you get them in the right spot. Sadly, it looks like I'm going to have to kill all of you now, too."

"Ha! How are you going to do that with one gun? There are seven of us," Ida pointed out.

"No worries. I have a plan that will put most of you out of commission before you even know what hit you." Endora slid the hand not holding the gun into the drawer. In lightning-fast moves, she whipped out several knives in quick succession.

Thwack!

Thwack!

Thwack!

Her aim was perfect, targeting Nans and the ladies right in the heart. Luckily, Nans and the ladies had lightning-fast moves themselves. Each of them whipped their patent leather purses up in front of their chests like a shiny shield.

The knives thudded into the purses, sticking straight out. Lexy held her breath, but the knives didn't penetrate.

The ladies looked down at their purses, surprise registering on their wrinkled faces.

"Wow, I knew these patent leather purses from Macy's were high quality, but this takes the cake!" Ruth said.

"Speaking of cake," Ida turned to Endora and said, "you brought corn muffins to Rosa, didn't you?"

Endora, who had been reaching into the drawer, probably for more knives, paused. "Yeah, so?"

"That's a big clue to the identity of the killer. The police know all about it. And there's a clue that points to you right in the dining room," Ida said

Endora faltered. "What do you mean?"

"The box from Sugar Daddies. Proves you frequent that shop, and I'm sure if the police go to that bakery and show them your picture, they will recognize you as having purchased corn muffins with sugar crystals on top." Ida looked her up and down. "You are, after all, rather memorable."

"That's right," Nans agreed. "So you better make sure to get rid of that evidence when you are getting rid of us."

The comment must have done the trick of distracting Endora because she seemed to forget all about the drawer. She kept the gun on them, though, so no one could make a move on her just yet, but Lexy knew that Nans had a plan.

"What box?" Endora asked.

"It's right there on the floor next to the server." Ida tilted her head toward the dining room.

Endora looked like she was considering the fact

that Ida could have been leading her on, but her curiosity about the box got the better of her. She stepped toward the dining room. When she was farther than arm's length from the knife drawer, Mario yelled out, "I've got her!"

With a speed and agility that belied his age, he leaped into the air and landed on Endora. The two of them thudded to the floor.

Crack! The gun went off, and Mario lay still on top of Endora.

Ruth rushed to his side. "Mario! Mario! Speak to me!"

"Get off of me!" Endora yelled as she wriggled and squirmed to get out from underneath Mario.

Finally, Mario moved, and Ruth breathed a sigh of relief. He tried to grab on to Endora, but his gnarled, weak arthritic hands had a hard time keeping hold of her while she kicked and beat at him.

"Out of the way!" William yelled. He spun and plucked the knife out of Nans's purse then aimed it at Mario.

"No!" Ruth yelled.

William threw the knife then quickly plucked the knives out of the other purses and threw them toward Mario and Endora.

At first, Lexy thought he was throwing them *at* Mario. Was he in cahoots with Endora? But as she peered around Nans's shoulder, she saw that wasn't the case at all. William had aimed expertly, and the knives had pierced only the material of Endora's jumpsuit, thus pinning her arms and legs down as if she were in a straitjacket.

William rushed over to help Mario up. "Are you okay, Uncle?"

"Yes, yes. Thank you, William." Mario patted William on the shoulder then turned to Nans and the ladies. "Ladies, I think I owe you an apology. I had no idea Endora was such a snake."

"Sorry that you had to find out this way." Ruth put a comforting hand on Mario's arm.

"And Helen, I apologize for moving the signs and following you." Mario looked down at Endora and shook his head. "That was all her idea. She said you were trying to get the murder charge against Henry dropped, and I couldn't have that. She had me convinced that Henry killed my granddaughter. I've done him a terrible disservice, and now I must make it right. If you will excuse me, I must get to the prison right away."

Helen glanced at her watch. "But the voting is in

one hour. Don't you want to be there to persuade those who haven't made up their minds yet?"

Mario opened the front door. "This is more important. I told the police I thought Henry was guilty, and the least I can do is make sure Henry doesn't spend one more minute in jail!" Mario opened the front door then turned to William. "Will you call the police and make sure Endora gets into their custody?"

"Of course, Uncle." Mario whipped out his phone and dialed 911.

"We'll stick around too, just in case," Ruth said.

Mario nodded and went out the door.

Ruth turned to Helen. "See, Mario isn't such a bad guy."

"Other than his choice in women." Helen glanced back at Endora, who was cursing and struggling on the floor. "But you and Mario might make a nice couple, now that he's single. I guess I really was wrong about him."

"You being wrong isn't what's important," Ruth said as the wail of sirens grew louder.

"What is?" Helen asked.

"That I was right."

"What's really important is that no one got hurt and we caught the killer," Nans said.

"No one got hurt? Then why is Ida's purse bleeding?" Lexy pointed to the purse, where a blob of red had oozed out and was dripping down the front.

Ida looked down. "Oh, darn!" She snapped the purse open and pulled out a red-stained napkin. "That knife went right into the middle of the jelly donut I had in my purse!"

CHAPTER 23

One week later...

The Brook Ridge Falls Retirement Center buzzed with excitement as Lexy rearranged the platters of pastries and cookies that were set up on the long tables lining one side of the room. It was Helen's first free-coffee Saturday since she'd been elected president of the community center, and she wanted everything to be perfect.

Lexy had offered to provide pastries at no cost as long as she could put a little card behind the trays with her bakery name and logo. Even if she wasn't making money on the baked goods, it would pay off. This kind of advertising was worth its weight in gold.

She'd loaded the tables with a good assortment of cookies, brownies, scones, and cupcakes. No corn muffins, though… they'd had enough of those.

"I think the black purse is more classic." Nans held her new purse up to show the ladies. They'd all gotten new purses after Endora had ruined their old ones with the knives.

"Maybe, but it's not suitable for all seasons." Ruth held her purse up. "I like beige because it goes with everything and can be used year-round. Black is too dark for summer."

"I think navy is smart and a little different. Not as formal as black but doesn't get as dirty as beige." Ida snapped her purse open and shoved a napkin-wrapped cookie inside. When she noticed everyone looking at her, she said, "What? I might need a little snack for later."

"No matter what color, they make good shields," Helen joked.

"Yeah, we know how to pull out all the stops," Ida said. "And I think we can safely say we cracked the case of Rosa Maguire's murder."

"And Helen still managed to get elected president

of the community center even though she spent a lot of time investigating the case," Nans said.

"Well, I do feel like I was the best person for the job, but it turns out Mario isn't so bad after all." Helen's gaze drifted past Lexy's shoulder. "Oh, here he comes. If you ladies will excuse me, I have an announcement to make."

Helen met Mario just inside the door, and the two of them shook hands and walked together to the front of the room.

"I wonder what she's up to," Nans said.

Ida shook her head. "Knowing Helen, it could be anything."

Ruth's forehead creased in concern. "Is she making an announcement with Mario? I hope they aren't getting married or anything."

"Attention! Attention!" Helen's loud voice hushed the crowd, and everyone turned toward her expectantly. "As many of you know, the unfortunate incident that resulted in the community center president vacancy also resulted in a vacancy for the office of treasurer."

The crowd mumbled and whispered. A few of them glanced back at Lexy, who busied herself with the pastries. Not that any of that had been her fault, but since both of those openings had stemmed from the community center president having been found dead in one of her pies, she was a little sensitive about it.

"As you know," Helen continued, "the position of treasurer is appointed by the president and I, as your newly elected president of the community center, appoint Mario Blondini as community center treasurer!"

The crowd applauded, and Mario shook Helen's hand, looking quite pleased with himself.

"Oh, well, that was nice of Helen." Ruth looked relived that the announcement wasn't of more of a personal nature.

"Looks like our opponents have become allies." Jack picked a brownie off the tray and gave Lexy a peck on the cheek.

"Hi, Jack." Nans tilted her cheek so he could give her a peck too. "Great to see you. Not working the weekend shift?"

"Nope. Got the day off, and I wanted to spend it with my wife."

"That's nice," Ida said. "I guess there's nothing for you to do now that we solved the Rosa Maguire case."

Jack frowned. "Well, I don't know if there's

nothing for me to do, but we did appreciate your help on that one."

"Actually, we solved three cases—Rosa's, Ruby's, and the Broadmoore heist," Helen said as she and Mario joined the circle. Lexy noticed that Ruth managed to maneuver so she was next to Mario.

"I want to thank you ladies again for finding my granddaughter's real killer." Mario shook his head. "I can't believe she had me convinced it was Henry."

"I knew it wasn't Henry all along." They all shuffled around to make room for Muriel and Henry Maguire. Muriel turned to Nans. "And I thank you ladies very much for proving it."

"And thank you, Mario, for coming straight to the prison as soon as you knew the truth," Henry said to Mario. "It means a lot."

Mario had rushed to the prison after they'd captured Endora, but of course, they didn't let Henry out on his say-so. Once Jack had relayed that they had a full confession in front of several witnesses, the paperwork was started, and Henry was released pretty quickly.

"We're happy that we could be a part of Henry's release. We certainly don't want to see an innocent man go to jail." Nans frowned at Henry. "There's just one thing that we never figured out."

"What's that?" Henry asked.

"Why did you lie about someone dying at the hospital that night, and where were you? There's is a gap in the timeline, so you must have gone somewhere, but you never said where," Nans said.

"Maybe it had to do with the scandal." Ida glanced at Muriel. "We never found out what that was either."

Henry's cheeks turned red, and he glanced around the circle. He looked like he was considering running off. Jack took notice, scrutinizing him carefully. Everyone leaned in as Henry opened his mouth to speak.

"It's true, I did lie about that night. I panicked because I couldn't let anyone find out where I really was. Lots of lives are at stake." Henry looked at them imploringly.

Ida scowled. "What in the world are you talking about? Spit it out."

Henry took a deep breath. "You see, I'm in an underground humanitarian effort. A few of the other doctors and I supply insulin to the homeless. That's the so-called scandal."

"You steal insulin from the hospital?" Ruth asked.

Henry shook his head. "Not steal. We buy it with our own money. But since buying it from the hospital that way is a special case, there was a glitch one time and it appeared as if some insulin was missing. We have a legal clinic designation, so buying it is all within regulation, but something got messed up."

"So what does that have to do with you lying about what happened that night?" Ida was still skeptical.

Henry leaned in and lowered his voice. "We take the insulin to the homeless people because they won't come in for treatment. A few of them are diabetic, and it's hard enough to get them to treat themselves. We do have an official clinic, and we're not supposed to be going out on the streets. All the doctors involved would lose their licenses. That's why I lied. I was protecting them. I'm only telling you now because you all worked hard to clear my name, and I trust you won't tell anyone." Henry looked at Jack.

"Sounds like you're doing a good deed. I'm going to forget all about it once I leave here," Jack said.

"Me too," Nans added.

The others echoed the same sentiment, and Henry relaxed.

"That explains the loitering charge, too," Nans said, and everyone nodded.

"So, everything has turned out as good as can be."

Mario's voice was cheery, but his face turned sad. "Except we can't bring Rosa or Ruby back."

"Unfortunately not," Ruth said.

"But we can look forward to new beginnings." Mario put one arm around Henry and the other around Ruth. "And to new friendships, trust, and the truth."

"Hear, hear!" Everyone raised their coffees in a mock toast.

Jack turned to Lexy. "Speaking of trust and the truth, do you have something to tell me?"

Lexy had procrastinated telling Jack about her visit to the prison. She wondered how he had even found out. Luckily, he didn't look mad.

"I might have a little something to discuss. Not that I went back on my word or anything, but maybe we had a miscommunication about a promise?" Lexy looked up at him from underneath her lashes.

"Oh, is that what it was? Okay, then maybe we should discuss that."

"Not here, later. I have a little idea on something that will make you forget all about our miscommunication." Lexy winked at Jack.

Jack's brows rose, and his honey-brown eyes took on a mischievous twinkle. He put his arm around her shoulders and led her away from the group. "Really? Do tell."

"It's something you really, really like."

"Tell me more."

"Your favorite double-chocolate eclairs."

Jack laughed. "That wasn't exactly what I had in mind, but I guess it's a start."

****

Sign up for my VIP reader list and get my books at the lowest discount price:
http://www.leighanndobbs.com/newsletter

Join my Facebook readers group and get special content and the inside scoop on my books:
https://www.facebook.com/groups/ldobbsreaders

If you want to receive a text message on your cell phone for new releases, text COZYMYSTERY to 88202 (sorry, this only works for US cell phones!)

Mummified Meringues

Brutal Brulee (Novella)

No Scone Unturned

Cream Puff Killer

Never Say Pie

Kate Diamond Mystery Adventures

***

Hidden Agemda (Book 1)

Ancient Hiss Story (Book 2)

Heist Society (Book 3)

Oyster Cove Guesthouse

Cat Cozy Mystery Series

***

A Twist in the Tail

A Whisker in the Dark

A Purrfect Alibi

Silver Hollow

Paranormal Cozy Mystery Series

***

A Spell of Trouble (Book 1)

Spell Disaster (Book 2)

Nothing to Croak About (Book 3)

Cry Wolf (Book 4)

Shear Magic (Book 5)

Mooseamuck Island

Cozy Mystery Series

* * *

A Zen For Murder

A Crabby Killer

A Treacherous Treasure

Mystic Notch

Cat Cozy Mystery Series

* * *

Ghostly Paws

A Spirited Tail

A Mew To A Kill

Paws and Effect

Probable Paws

Whisker of a Doubt

Wrong Side of the Claw

Blackmoore Sisters

Cozy Mystery Series

* * *

Dead Wrong

Dead & Buried

Dead Tide

Buried Secrets

Deadly Intentions

A Grave Mistake

Spell Found

Fatal Fortune

Hidden Secrets

Hazel Martin Historical Mystery Series

***

Murder at Lowry House (book 1)

Murder by Misunderstanding (book 2)

Lady Katherine Regency Mysteries

***

An Invitation to Murder (Book 1)

The Baffling Burglaries of Bath (Book 2)

Sam Mason Mysteries

(As L. A. Dobbs)

***

Telling Lies (Book 1)

Keeping Secrets (Book 2)

Exposing Truths (Book 3)

Betraying Trust (Book 4)

Contemporary Romance

***

Reluctant Romance

Sweet Romance (Written As Annie Dobbs)

Firefly Inn Series

***

Another Chance (Book 1)

Another Wish (Book 2)

Hometown Hearts Series

***

No Getting Over You (Book 1)

A Change of Heart (Book 2)

Romantic Comedy

***

Corporate Chaos Series

In Over Her Head (book 1)

Can't Stand the Heat (book 2)

What Goes Around Comes Around (book 3)

Careful What You Wish For (4)

***

Sweetrock Sweet and Spicy Cowboy Romance

Some Like It Hot

Too Close For Comfort

———

Regency Romance

* * *

Scandals and Spies Series:

Kissing The Enemy

Deceiving the Duke

Tempting the Rival

Charming the Spy

Pursuing the Traitor

Captivating the Captain

The Unexpected Series:

An Unexpected Proposal

An Unexpected Passion

Dobbs Fancytales:

Dobbs Fancytales Boxed Set Collection

————

Western Historical Romance

***

Goldwater Creek Mail Order Brides:

Faith

American Mail Order Brides Series:

Chevonne: Bride of Oklahoma

————————

Magical Romance with a Touch of Mystery

***

Something Magical

Curiously Enchanted

ROMANTIC SUSPENSE
WRITING AS LEE ANNE JONES:

***

The Rockford Security Series:

Deadly Betrayal (Book 1)

Fatal Games (Book 2)

Treacherous Seduction (Book 3)

Calculating Desires (Book 4)

Wicked Deception (Book 5)

USA Today bestselling author, Leighann Dobbs, discovered her passion for writing after a twenty year career as a software engineer. She lives in New Hampshire with her husband Bruce, their trusty Chihuahua mix Mojo and beautiful rescue cat, Kitty. When she's not reading, gardening, making jewelry or selling antiques, she likes to write cozy mystery and historical romance books.

Her book "Dead Wrong" won the "Best Mystery Romance" award at the 2014 Indie Romance Convention.

Her book "Ghostly Paws" was the 2015 Chanticleer Mystery & Mayhem First Place category winner in the Animal Mystery category.

Find out about her latest books by signing up at:

http://www.leighanndobbs.com/newsletter

Connect with Leighann on Facebook
http://facebook.com/leighanndobbsbooks

Join her VIP readers group on Facebook:
https://www.facebook.com/groups/ldobbsreaders/